She had to plan

With an enormous, life-changing agenda ahead of her, Kathleen was overwhelmed. So she started with the obvious.

What to wear?

She wanted to look sexy but not cheap. Stylish but not unapproachable.

"What am I doing?" Kathleen turned away from the mirror. Plotting Zachary Foster's seduction, dressing herself like bait for a trap. How shallow!

She'd changed in the past year. Before, she'd been more than a little spoiled. But now, she knew the depths of sorrow. She'd leapt back in time, hoping to make Foster fall in love with her and revise their tortured past. Yet she wasn't quite sure whether manipulating him into bed was fair.

"Later," she promised herself. She'd think about ethics later. Right now, the clock was ticking. She had twenty-four hours to take action...

Or she'd lose this precious second chance at love...forever.

ABOUT THE AUTHOR

Cassie Miles lives in Denver with her two teenage daughters. She's written many Harlequin novels and has long been a steady contributor to the Intrigue series. While she continues to write romantic mysteries for Harlequin Intrigue, she was pleased to pen her first American Romance, *Buffalo McCloud*, in January of 1995. *Borrowed Time* is her second book for the series.

Books by Cassie Miles

HARLEQUIN AMERICAN ROMANCE
567—BUFFALO McCLOUD

HARLEQUIN INTRIGUE
122—HIDE AND SEEK
150—HANDLE WITH CARE
237—HEARTBREAK HOTEL
269—ARE YOU LONESOME TONIGHT?
285—DON'T BE CRUEL

HARLEQUIN TEMPTATION
161—ACTS OF MAGIC
204—IT'S ONLY NATURAL
270—SEEMS LIKE OLD TIMES
335—MONKEY BUSINESS
405—UNDER LOCK AND KEY
494—A RISKY PROPOSITION

Cassie Miles

BORROWED TIME

BORROWED TIME

All rights reserved. Except for use in any review, the reproduction or utilization of this work in whole or in part in any form by any electronic, mechanical or other means, now known or hereafter invented, including xerography, photocopying and recording, or in any information storage or retrieval system, is forbidden without the written permission of the publisher, Harlequin Enterprises Limited, 225 Duncan Mill Road, Don Mills, Ontario, Canada M3B 3K9.

All characters in this book have no existence outside the imagination of the author and have no relation whatsoever to anyone bearing the same name or names. They are not even distantly inspired by any individual known or unknown to the author, and all incidents are pure invention.

This edition published by arrangement with Harlequin Books S.A.

® and TM are trademarks of the publisher. Trademarks indicated with ® are registered in the United States Patent and Trademark Office, the Canadian Trade Marks Office and in other countries.

Harlequin Books

TORONTO • NEW YORK • LONDON
AMSTERDAM • PARIS • SYDNEY • HAMBURG
STOCKHOLM • ATHENS • TOKYO • MILAN
MADRID • WARSAW • BUDAPEST • AUCKLAND

ISBN 0-373-16574-9

BORROWED TIME

Prologue

So far, this had been one of the worst days in her life.

That morning, around ten o'clock, Kathleen Welles had had a horrendous but totally predictable argument with her mother. Recently, Hannah Welles had become obsessed with seeing her only daughter get married and have children to carry on the Welles dynasty. Worse, Hannah had the gall to insist that Kathleen leave off her "wrongheaded infatuation" with that "social reprobate," Zachary Foster.

The ensuing fight had not been pretty.

After she stormed away from her mother's harangue, Kathleen put in an appearance at her own plush downtown Denver office, where she worked as a fashion buyer for the Welles department store. The family business. Her mother was president, CEO, majority stockholder. The decision maker and planner. Kathleen was...bored silly.

As usual, she found nothing to do. So she left her office and rummaged through the incredible inventory in the shoe department, but she still couldn't find the right shade of purple to match her favorite silk blouse.

Meandering past the beauty salon on the second floor, she decided to do something new with her hair. Shoulder-length was way too hot for summer. But her favorite stylist was totally booked.

Then Kathleen's luncheon date up and canceled, without so much as a by-your-leave.

A perfectly dreadful day!

But this afternoon promised to be better. At quarter to three, she slipped behind the wheel of her BMW and headed southeast toward Zachary Foster's studio. He'd called and said he had a surprise for her. Finally, something good was coming her way.

In Foster's quiet Capitol Hill neighborhood, she made a sharp right, zipped down the alley and squeezed into a space right outside his carriage house. In a few strides, she was knocking at the door, certain that her day was about to improve significantly. "Foster, it's me. I'm here."

He opened the door and leaned against the frame. "What's the secret password?"

The word *handsome* sprang to her lips, but she didn't say it out loud. No sense in stroking a man's vanity. But, oh, my, this man was gorgeous. Tall and lean, with Levi's slung low on his hips. He wore a blue work shirt, unbuttoned in the June heat, and Kathleen's gaze was instantly drawn to his muscular chest with its enticing sprinkling of dark hair. She sighed and looked up at his face. He hadn't shaved. His long brown hair was, as always, a little unkempt. He looked back at her, his penetrating blue eyes seeming to probe her very mind and plant erotic thoughts there.

"Come on, Kathleen. You don't get in until you say the password."

"I don't know it."

"Take a guess."

She rolled her brown eyes heavenward and picked a word at random. "Cantaloupe."

He nodded. "Enter, princess."

"Into your kingdom?" she asked sardonically.

"An artist's studio is his castle," he paraphrased.

She sidled past him, and as she brushed fleetingly against his chest, she felt the temperature on this summery day rise several degrees.

Despite what her mother thought, they weren't dating. But there was definitely something between them, and their flirtation had escalated to a dangerously sensual level. Kathleen toyed with the idea of taking the next step. Moving beyond a few casual kisses to... something more. A lot more.

Quickly, she turned her attention back to his studio. Foster's artistic domain always delighted her. From the outside, his carriage house looked small as a cottage. Within, the high windows and two skylights created an airy spaciousness. There was a tiny galley kitchen and bathroom. The sleeping area was a loft. The rest of the interior was devoted to art. Even with the windows open, the distinctive scent of oils and turpentine tickled her nostrils.

Kathleen's portrait was, she knew, only one of his current projects, but he'd told her, again and again, that the paintings he'd done of her—one oil and two acrylics—represented his best work ever. She'd been posing, off and on, for nearly two months.

She lowered herself onto the futon sofa, one of the few pieces of actual furniture in his studio, and allowed her gaze to wander. Paintings and frames leaned against the white walls. Three easels held canvases of varying sizes, each covered by a drop cloth.

Foster stood before them and gestured grandly. "Your surprise."

"Three white sheets," she teased. "Gosh, thanks a heap."

"Beneath those sheets are the finest paintings I've ever done. Portraits of you. The best model I've ever had."

"Better than models in New York City?" She batted her eyelashes, shamelessly fishing for compliments. "Better than in Paris?"

"New York. Paris. San Francisco. Milan. I had to travel around the world to realize that the most beautiful woman was right here in Denver, my hometown."

A thrill chased up and down her spine. The most beautiful woman in the world? His lavish praise excited her, as did the reminder of a worldliness far different than her own, born of broad, exotic experience rather than of wealth and privilege. "Then I guess it was worth it for me to . . . get undressed."

"When you came here, I know you wanted a sedate pose. But I didn't see you that way." His blue eyes flared like butane flames. "I thank you for indulging my vision."

"Well, may I see the paintings now?"

"There's something I want to tell you first."

"Yes?" She waited expectantly.

He broke their intense eye contact and began pacing, as she'd often seen him do when frustrated with his painting. He moved with unceasing, restless grace.

"Foster, is something bothering you?"

"Yes and no." Zach had never expected his interest in Kathleen Welles to reach this point, a boiling point. Though she inspired him as an artist, for various reasons she wasn't his number-one choice as a model. Her personality, her social status as the Welles heiress created complications. And now, he needed her cooperation. She simply had to go along with his plan.

"Let me see the paintings," she demanded.

"Not yet." How could he explain? In his regular—paying—job as the owner of a window-design company, Zach worked for Kathleen's department store. That was how they'd met. Otherwise, he never would have come into contact with her. They traveled in different circles. Different classes. Different worlds, he thought. She was a princess. He was little more than a pauper.

"Tomorrow night," he started explaining, "I have a showing at Kendall Gallery."

"I know. I'm planning to be there." She beamed at him. "Everybody who's anybody will be there. It's going to be quite an event. Four promising artists, all local."

"Only three," he said. "One of them had to drop out."

"That's a shame. This showing could really put Denver on the map as an artistic community and make you all a ton of money." Her lovely face drew into a frown. "This doesn't mean you're going to close down your company, does it?"

"No."

"I'm so glad. Because I love what you do for Welles."

He stood before her, then looked directly into her rich brown eyes. Dancing eyes, he thought, so full of life. Pleasure seeking. Hedonistic. Despite her wealth and station, Kathleen was something of a free spirit. He could see it in her, even submerged, as it was, by the conformity demanded by her class.

Taking her perfectly manicured hands in his own, he said, "I'm going to ask a favor of you. A big favor."

"Okay." She wanted to promise him anything, but something warned her to hold back. He seemed so serious.

"As I said, these studies of you are my best work to date. Perhaps the best I'll ever do. Because one of the artists dropped out, there's more space at the gallery. I'd like to display these paintings."

"My portraits?" She was delighted, flattered beyond belief.

Then uncertainty set in. Foster seemed awfully nervous about something. "The people coming to the show know me. They'll recognize me in your paintings," she said, pointedly.

"And they'll be enchanted. As I am."

He'd answered too fast. She definitely had something to worry about. She pulled her hands away from him, dread dousing her earlier excitement. "Let me see them."

Suspiciously, she watched as he went to the first easel. He had never allowed her to view his work in progress. Now she was immensely curious...but strangely afraid.

He removed the sheet from the smallest painting. In blue and mauve and rose tones, she saw her long black hair, her forehead, her wide open eyes, her uplifted chin, her throat...and her bare breasts.

The second work showed her face, eyes demurely downcast. And her naked torso.

In the third, he'd painted her entire body, slender as a taper. And nude.

"They're..." she began in a whisper, for once in her life at a loss for words.

"A celebration of the female form," he said. "There's a wonderful fluidity in the way you hold yourself," he added with maddening—and wholly inappropriate, considering the circumstances—objectivity.

"But—but I was never completely nude."

"Close enough." He grinned. "It wasn't hard to imagine the rest."

She pushed herself off the futon and neared the paintings. They seemed to take on a life of their own. Was that really her? Was she so dramatic, so intense, so fascinating? Despite her shock, and despite the oddly unsettling intimacy of the moment, Kathleen was enthralled at the obvious artistry. "Oh, Foster. These are wonderful," she breathed.

"I know."

The depth in the paintings amazed her. Though she and Foster had exchanged only a few incredible, heart-stopping kisses, these works displayed an astonishing sense of intimacy. It was as if he'd penetrated her very soul.

"I want to show them at the gallery tomorrow," he repeated.

She whirled to face him. "But—but you can't! No way. Not a chance."

It was as he'd feared. Though Kathleen Welles fancied herself daring, a risk taker, her risks were always minimal ones, minor rebellions circumscribed by a safety net of money and prestige.

"But, Kathleen, this is art," he asserted.

"This is me! Naked! I'm not about to put my body on display for the entire city of Denver to stare at."

Though Kathleen had never thought of herself as prim—why, she'd posed in her undies, hadn't she?— a curious shame at such public exposure suddenly

overcame her. Every social stricture ever drummed
into her head came to the fore. Why, if Denver society viewed these pictures, the embarrassment would be
overwhelming. Too easily, she imagined the snicker-
ing when people recognized her as Foster's model.
Everyone in town would know that she had sat, nearly
naked, for hours in the presence of a socially dubious
male. Everyone would know that Kathleen Welles had
three moles forming a small triangle below her left
breast! She would never be able to face her friends
again. And her mother? If these pictures were displayed, Hannah Welles would have a heart attack.

"I need to do this, Kathleen."

"No, you don't. *I'll* buy the paintings from you.
Right now." She went to the futon and grabbed her
purse. "Name your price."

"This isn't about money." He came to her, held her
by the shoulders. "Try to see this from my perspective. I've been painting for fourteen years. Nothing
I've done comes close to these three works. I want
them to be seen."

"Can't you—can't you change them? Make my hair
blond or something?"

"They're perfect. I wouldn't touch them for the
world."

She broke free from his grasp, pushed away from
him. How could he do this to her? How could he ex-
pose her for everyone to see? "You can't do this."

"Actually, I can. I'm within my rights as an artist
to offer any of my creative works for sale."

"Someone else could buy them? A painting of my naked body could be in someone else's home?"

"Technically, yes. But if you don't want me to sell them, I won't."

"A fat lot of good that will do. These studies are brilliant! People will remember them."

"I hope so."

A frantic anger roiled and surged within her as all the possible consequences unfurled before her horrified mind's eye. Though known for her hot temper, she fought to control it. This matter was too serious for a tantrum. "What if you become famous? What if these portraits are reproduced? Turned into posters, postcards?"

"That would be great. Imagine it." He tried for lightness. "You could be hanging in a museum, as famous as the *Mona Lisa.*"

"She had all her clothes on!"

"You're being provincial," he said. "People will see this as art. Not as you."

She felt violated. She had trusted him when he talked her into slipping her blouse off her shoulders, then stripping to her flesh-colored bra and silk panties. And then, just once, she'd removed her bra. Foster had been utterly respectful, almost remote, not at all lecherous. He had never tried to touch her. So posing nearly naked had seemed like a lark. Slightly naughty but safe. Never had she expected to be put on display. "No!" she shouted. "I won't let you do this to me!"

"Try to understand—" he began.

His soothing tone infuriated her. "Listen, Foster, I'm not some little bimbo off the street. People know who I am. I have a position in the community, and I will not be humiliated."

"But you're beautiful in these portraits."

"Save it." She jabbed her forefinger against his chest. "You go to hell, Foster. You're not going to sweet-talk me into this."

He grabbed her wrist. "Look, this is about me, not you. This is about fourteen years of work. My life-work."

She yanked away from him. With her free hand, she took a swing at him, which he managed to duck. Her temper now consumed her. How dare he? "No!" she screamed. "No! I won't let you!"

She flung herself at the table where he kept his paints and tools. She grasped his X-Acto knife, the small razor-sharp instrument with which he cut canvas, and brandished it wildly.

"Kathleen, stop!"

He caught her from behind, encircled her with his arms. Gently, he restrained her. "Calm down, Kathleen. Hush now. Calm down."

She fought him with all her strength. With all the bloodred fury of her infamous temper, she struggled against his grasp. But she was unable to break free.

Finally, a darkly clever idea penetrated her rage, and with cruel calculation, she went limp. She would get her way. Nothing would stop her.

Fighting the harsh anger that grated in her throat, she assumed a calm tone. "You can let me go now."

His grasp loosened. "Are you okay?"

"I'm fine."

With a pained wince, he released her and gingerly fingered his left side. "Dammit, Kathleen. I think you broke one of my ribs."

"Good!"

She spun around, and before he could react, she'd flown away from him and begun slashing at the canvases. He caught up with her at the last one, but, oddly, he did not try to stop her.

Breathing hard, she savagely plunged the blade into her painted throat and twisted, slashed, destroying the final canvas.

Finally, the blade dropped from her shaking hand.

And immediately, she was sorry for what she had done. What had come over her? She'd acted like an insane woman. Vicious, spoiled, impossible.

Gasping, she stared at Zachary Foster. Pure hatred shone in his gaze. His lips were curled in disgust.

She stumbled back a few steps.

"Here, Kathleen." He went to the futon, picked up her purse and threw it at her. "Don't forget your money."

He turned away from her, his shoulders slumped. He looked defeated, abject, as if he had lost a loved one.

And he had, she realized. These paintings had life to him. In his mind, her actions were doubtless equivalent to murder.

Apologies would never suffice. She could never make up for what she'd done.

It was too late.

Chapter One

The hot-pink flier with bold chartreuse lettering radiated a tackiness that was out of place in the otherwise tasteful office of Kathleen Welles. "I Buy Time," the gaudy brochure proclaimed. "Any Day, Past or Present. Top Dollar. Big Bucks."

Kathleen creased the circular carefully and slipped it into her purse. Other matters required her immediate attention. She strode from her office on the eighth floor of the Welles department store and paused at her secretary's desk. "Helen, do you have the—"

"Contracts for you to sign? Of course." Ever-efficient, Helen produced the paperwork and a pen. "Congratulations. You always were good at negotiations."

"Well, I do love a bargain." As had become almost second nature over the past year, Kathleen filled in her signature above the line marked "President, Welles, Incorporated." She'd worked out a very good deal with the cash-register people, but it had taken four weeks of meetings and innumerable lunches. "I'm glad this is over. I'll be—"

"Going to lunch" Helen completed her sentence.

"And I might be a little—"

"Late," her secretary said. "You haven't forgotten that problem with the window dressers, have you?"

"I'll speak with Zach Foster on my way out." *Zach Foster. Zachary Emile Foster.* His name pounded in her brain like an echo across a mile-deep canyon. But this sound never faded to silence. Instead, the resonance grew louder and more intense. *Foster, Foster. Dammit. Won't you ever forgive and forget?*

Kathleen pressed her lips together, holding back her sighs, her moans, her cries. Every time she saw him or thought of him, she felt a sharp pain beneath her rib cage. It was as if her dormant heart, unable to love any other man, remembered Foster and would not cease to ache. Her sorrow had not lessened in the year since the disastrous end of their relationship. Their stillborn relationship, she thought. She never even had a chance to know—

"Kathleen? Are you all right?" Helen asked.

All right? Hardly. Her life was empty and miserable. She'd been so foolish. She'd thrown away her only chance at love. Real love. Eternal love. "I'm fine."

"You'll find Foster down on the first floor. He's working in the left front window."

"Thank you."

"Frankly, I'd consider replacing him if I were you," Helen chided as she tucked a wisp of silvery gray hair behind her ear. "There are other window-display contractors in town."

Kathleen didn't bother to argue.

"He looks like a thug," Helen continued. "Half the time he doesn't shave, and his hair is too long. Some of his helpers have tattoos. I mean, really, Kathleen, the salesclerks are probably afraid of him."

"Afraid?" That wasn't Kathleen's impression. Every time Zachary Foster was around, she heard feminine giggles and saw blushing cheeks. Most of the female clerks seemed hot for the contractor's body, longing to run their fingers through his thick, slightly shaggy brown hair and nuzzle up against his unshaven jaw.

"He doesn't look like a window dresser," Helen mused.

"No, he doesn't."

"But he's sure temperamental. Acts like he's an artist or something."

"He is an artist," Kathleen said softly. A better artist than anyone knew. Kathleen alone had seen his masterpieces. And she had destroyed them. There was no doubt that she'd set him back considerably in his artistic career.

"I say he's trouble," said Helen. She turned back to her computer terminal and poked vigorously at the keyboard, still complaining. "Foster and his tattooed sidekicks look like Hell's Angels. Have you seen that boy, Donny?"

"The one with the earrings and the Mega-Death tattoo?"

"Nothing but trouble," Helen muttered. "If your mother were still running things, she wouldn't put up with Zachary Foster."

That was another argument Kathleen did not choose to pursue. She and her mother, Hannah Welles, had very different ways of doing things. It had taken months to convince the employees at Welles that Kathleen would not lead them directly into disaster when her mother was incapacitated with a stroke and Kathleen took over as acting president.

As she navigated through the offices to the elevators, her long strides rippled the full skirt of her black jersey dress. If it weren't for its sleeveless top, the coal black outfit might have looked like mourning attire. And perhaps it was. For she was still grieving the events that had occurred exactly one year ago today, June twenty-first.

If only she could erase that day, pretend it had never happened. Life could be so very different....

Maybe Helen was right. Maybe she should hire another, less disturbing, contractor to do the windows. But Zachary Foster's work was excellent. How could she fire him when he did such a good job? If there was one thing Kathleen had learned in this long, horrible year, it was the importance of being responsible. Her primary concern was to do what was best for Welles. This elegant downtown Denver store was the last of its breed on the Sixteenth Street Mall, and she was determined not to sell out to a chain or give up the splendid eight-story building with white cornices and marbled entryway. Preserve the dinosaur, she thought. This high-class beast did not deserve extinction.

On the first floor, she strode past leather purses, silk scarves and the glitter of faux and real jewels and slipped through a door into the narrow corridor behind the left front display window.

And there he was.

"Hello, Kathleen."

Her aching heart thudded. Her mouth was suddenly dry as the Sahara. He was so broad-shouldered that he filled the tiny space behind the window. "Hello, Foster."

"Don't you look... stark. A study in black and white."

At one time, he'd told her she was beautiful. He'd complimented her fair skin and the black hair she'd recently cut into a chin-length bob. Now, when she looked into his blue eyes, she saw only a cold reflection, the radiance of a woman in love lost.

Business, she reminded herself. She was here to talk business, not to reminisce. "I was told there was a problem with the display."

"It's the jewelry. This stuff is junk. I'll show you."

She followed him, sliding her hand against the wall behind the display and trying to remain cool. Helen was wrong about Foster. He wasn't a thug. But he was aggressively masculine, with his Levi's riding low on his hips and the sleeveless T-shirt he wore working under the hot display lights. That he hadn't shaved in a couple of days somehow emphasized the granite squareness of his jawline.

In the window, he scooped up a handful of glittering baubles. "Junk," he said. "I need to use real diamonds to achieve the effect we're after, but I need your authorization. So tell your lackeys it's okay, and I'll get on with my work."

Holding a fistful of fancy fake jewels, he looked like a swashbuckling pirate. A very dangerous man. Kathleen blinked to erase the image.

"Real diamonds will capture the light and make it dance," he said. "Imitations, no matter how good, won't do."

"You expect me to put real diamond jewelry on display in this window?"

"Yes."

"I can't do that," she said reasonably. "We don't have adequate security in this area."

A muscle twitched in his jaw. He was angry. Too angry for the situation, she thought. He dropped the costume jewelry, none too gently, and scowled at one of the mannequins. "It's your store. Do what you want."

"Better that you whistle and I fetch thousands of dollars' worth of precious gems? Like that, huh?" She snapped her fingers. "Well, think again. I'm not doing something I would surely regret."

He tilted a mannequin's head to the left. "Didn't think you were capable of regret, Kathleen."

How could he say that? Didn't he understand at all? Even now, when he was behaving like a temperamental, artistic jerk, she was regretting losing him. Every day, every minute, she relived the mistakes of those twenty-four hours—the day when she committed the unforgivable madness of destroying his art. Destroying their budding relationship.

She had never known how deeply she cared for him until she'd lost him forever. "God, yes. I have regrets."

He turned and faced her. "A princess like you? Heiress to the Welles fortune? I thought you were strictly out for fun."

"Fun?" Her mind was a million miles from laughter. "A princess?"

What was going on here? Every time she'd spoken to him during the past year, he'd been cold and reserved. Now he seemed to be attacking her. With a jolt, Kathleen realized that he might also be thinking of the events of one year ago.

"I need diamonds," he repeated. "The real stuff. I'm sick of fakes."

"So am I. I'm sick to death of people who don't say what they really mean. Tell me, Foster. What's your real problem?"

For an instant, they looked into each other's eyes. She saw his fire, his passion. But no forgiveness. Her guilt nearly overwhelmed her, but she did not look away. "I have another appointment. We'll talk about this after lunch."

"Two o'clock," he said. "Back here."

She fled through the corridor behind the display and headed for the exit, looking neither left nor right. Her emotions jarred around her in clumsy turmoil. She was on the street, then on the shuttle bus going north-west. At the Market Street station, she double-checked the address on the hot-pink flier. She was probably crazy to believe the gaudy print. "I Buy Time. Any Day, Past or Present."

Of course, the claim was impossible. It had to be a joke or a scam. And Kathleen questioned her common sense in even coming here. But the brochure had simply appeared on her desk, without envelope or return address, and somehow it beckoned to her. Was she being ridiculous?

On the other hand, why not take a chance? Burdened with responsibilities and bereft of love, she had nothing to lose.

The address laid beyond the many renovated and trendy lofts downtown, in an area that was still seedy and run-down. She scanned the old brick warehouse. Four arched windows lined the second floor. Across the flat roof was a jagged parapet from which stone gargoyles with broken noses sneered down at her, seeming to taunt her. She almost turned around and went back to her office. But by now she was too curious. And, possibly, a little bit desperate.

When she pressed the bell, a heavy wooden door buzzed open, and she stepped into the foyer. At least the inside of this decrepit building was clean. Black and white honeycomb tiles had been scrubbed and waxed to a shine. Two large clocks, perfectly synchronized, were mounted on opposite walls like a pair of ticking earmuffs. At the top of a long staircase was the silhouette of a woman wearing flowing scarves and dramatic ankle-length skirts.

"Welcome" came her melodic voice. "I'm Diana Marie Casey. Please come up."

At the top of the stairway, Kathleen entered a vast room boasting timepieces of every shape and description. Grandfather clocks, cuckoo clocks and a row of metronomes on shelves. There were square, digital faces and round clocks with fancy Roman numerals. By the four windows were sundials. The ticktock noises mimicked the twitter of birds. From somewhere among them came a chiming, marking the quarter hour past noon.

Kathleen was relieved to see a businesslike desk, even though, behind it, Diana Marie Casey was flamboyantly attired in layers of gauzy, rainbow-striped material and glittering bangles. Her long black hair was tied back with flowing scarves. As a fashion statement, Ms. Casey was definitely retro.

On one corner of her desk stood an ornate hourglass two feet tall. The frame was polished rosewood. The sands, flowing in a spiral through the narrow glass middle, shone like gold dust.

"Shall we get right down to business?" Diana Marie said. "Please sit. We don't have much time."

In view of all these clocks, her statement held a certain irony. Kathleen perched on a brocaded chair, determined not to prejudge until she'd heard what the woman's offer entailed.

"I am a time merchant," Diana Marie said. "I buy and sell time in twenty-four-hour blocks, from midnight to midnight. Now, are you interested in buying or selling?"

"I'm interested in changing one day," Kathleen admitted in spite of all logic. She studied the other woman carefully, noticing a glimmer of sharp intelligence in the depths of her coal black eyes. "Can you do that?"

"It's not customary."

"But not impossible? I want to go back in time, knowing what I know now, and relive one day in my past."

"Too complicated."

"Why?"

"Your actions could have an effect on other people. You could change destiny and cause all sorts of embarrassment. Why not just sell me the day? I pay big bucks, top dollar."

"Excuse me," Kathleen said, "but is it customary for a mystical, occult person such as yourself to talk like a used-car saleswoman?"

"I'm mercenary, like every other business person, my dear," she said, as if that explained everything. "Surely, you've heard the phrase, 'Cross my palm with silver, and I'll read your fortune.'"

"As in crystal balls?" Kathleen asked.

"Not anymore, honey. I run a complex business here." She smiled broadly. "Fully computerized."

"What's the catch?"

"No catch. Now which will it be? Buy or sell?"

Kathleen was still skeptical. "And what do you do with the time you buy from me? Resell it to someone else?"

"Perhaps."

"May I ask for references?"

"I'm sure you can understand that the identities of my clients are strictly private." Her laughter was low and musical. "What's the matter, dear? Don't you believe me?"

"Your proposition *is* unusual."

"But completely legitimate. As a business woman yourself," she said, evidently sizing up Kathleen's demeanor and attire, "you must understand. No doubt you buy time from your employees every day." She turned her head toward the hourglass and lovingly trailed her fingers down the smooth rosewood frame. "I advise you to make a decision quickly. My offer is good for only one hour, and we've already wasted seventeen minutes."

"You can tell that by reading an hourglass?" That was too much to believe. "I'm sorry, Ms. Casey, but—"

"I suppose a small demonstration is in order," the woman conceded. "Think of last Sunday, and stand."

As Kathleen warily rose to her feet, there was a deafening roar and a flash of brilliant white light. She was in the mountains, just as she had been last Sunday. But this wasn't a dream or hallucination. The details were too real. She heard the ripple of a creek, felt the wind in her hair, smelled the scent of piñon trees.

Her knees went weak. When she lowered herself to sit, she was back in the office, sitting in the chair opposite the desk.

With a smug grin, Diana Marie confronted her. "Are you satisfied now that I'm telling the truth?"

Gasping for breath, Kathleen rested her hand at her throat. For an instant, she'd actually flashed back in time. Was she crazy? Had she been hypnotized? "How did you do that?"

"It's possible to pop back and forth across the barriers of time. In a sort of time bubble. You've heard of déjà vu? Synchronicity?"

Kathleen nodded. "But is the past simultaneous with the present and the future? How can they happen at once?"

"Please, dear, let's leave the explanation of the time and space continuum to Einstein and the Stephen Hawkings. Now, I assume you'll sell. I suspect you have a day that you regret."

"Doesn't everyone?" She fought to control her accelerated pulse and to calm her breathing. She could go back in time! She could have a second chance!

"But you, especially, have made mistakes," said Diana Marie. "There was one day when you behaved like a spoiled princess. And you ruined everything."

Kathleen's cheeks warmed with guilty awareness. One year ago today, she'd fought with her mother, then vented her anger on Foster. In both cases, the consequences were terrible. She had destroyed Foster's art and ended their relationship. And later that day, when Kathleen went to her mother's home, hoping to make peace, Hannah had collapsed. Though Kathleen had felt certain she'd caused her mother's stroke, the doctors insisted that aneurysms were simply biological realities and that it was, in fact, fortunate Kathleen was there with her and had acted quickly in summoning aid. They said she'd saved her mother's life.

What if she hadn't been there? Would her mother have died? She couldn't take the chance of removing herself from that day in time. "I'm not interested in selling."

"Sell the day. Or live with the regrets."

But she couldn't. The stakes were too high. If she hadn't been there, her mother might have died. Still, she couldn't resist the opportunity to repair her past. And Kathleen was good at negotiations. There might be a way....

She sat up straight in the chair. Her features were utterly calm, betraying none of the eagerness she felt in her heart. "I wish to buy a day."

"Do you? How odd. Most often, the people who wish to purchase time are those facing imminent demise."

The chiming of a clock indicated another quarter of an hour had sped by. Time seemed to be moving faster than usual, minutes slipping by like seconds. Kathleen took her checkbook from her purse. "I'll give you a thousand dollars for one day."

"Why? You have unlimited days stretched ahead of you. Why would you purchase another?"

"Call it a savings account, for contingencies." Trying to sound rational in the face of this bizarre transaction, she added, "It would be reassuring to know that I always have one more tomorrow."

Diana Marie rose from behind the desk, paused beside the quickly emptying hourglass, then glided toward the arched windows. A neat row of gold clocks on a low shelf seemed to turn their faces toward her. She patted them fondly, as a mother would the heads of her small children, offering reassurance. "You're up to something," she said. "I advise you to be very careful. My offer is not to be taken lightly."

"Surely you understand," Kathleen said. "Time is so precious. I'd like to buy twenty-four hours."

"Half a million dollars. That's the going rate."

"Five thousand, and not a penny more."

"Four hundred thousand."

As their bargaining began in earnest, the Gypsy-like woman's eyes grew bright. Kathleen made another offer. Diana Marie countered. Back and forth. Back and forth. Finally, they settled on the sum of seventy-five thousand dollars. Quickly, Kathleen wrote the check and held it out. "I'll have to do some juggling this afternoon, but the check is good."

"Very pretty," Diana Marie said, reading the check. "Very pretty, indeed."

Kathleen scribbled a small note in the front corner of the check before handing it over. "It's a lot of money," she stressed.

"Certainly," Diana Marie agreed. She seemed ephemeral and transparent as she fondled the check. "Congratulations, you are now the owner of—"

"June twenty-first, one year ago," Kathleen said firmly. "That is the precise day I wish to buy."

"But that day has already occurred. You cannot—"

"You've accepted my check, and I wrote that date on the front side of the check." She pointed. "See? Under 'Purpose,' it says purchase of June twenty-first, one year ago."

"So it does."

"That's our contract. The day I wish to purchase is one year ago today. It's actually a bargain for you, Ms. Casey, because it was my day to begin with. And you're money ahead." The clocks chimed again, more loudly than before. "Time's almost up, Ms. Casey. Would you prefer that I tear up this check and cancel our deal?"

"You think you're sly, don't you?"

"I'm desperate," Kathleen admitted. "Please, Diana Marie. Give me this chance."

"I certainly hope this isn't about a man. If I had a penny for every woman who thought she might have a shot at eternal love, I'd retire a wealthy woman. It's all a lie, you know. Nothing lasts forever."

"Please. Let me try."

"It's interesting...." Diana Marie smiled, but with something other than amusement. "All right, Miss Welles, you have your day. You will go back in time to one year ago at midnight. At the stroke of the next midnight, you will return to the present."

"And the present will be altered by the changes I make on that day?"

"No guarantees! The events of June twenty-first one year ago might just as well have occurred on the following day or the next. Perhaps everything will be exactly as it is right now. Perhaps not. It might be worse."

For a moment, anxiety crowded Kathleen's mind. No guarantees? This might all be for nothing. She might be reexperiencing the worst pain in her life for nothing.

The sands filtered quickly through the glass. Almost gone. The chance was almost gone. Kathleen had to seize this opportunity. "I'm ready."

"So be it."

When Diana Marie stood beside her, the woman's skirts billowed as if she were standing on a windy shore instead of in an office. There was a chill in the air. A noise like cascading water sounded more loudly than the ticking of the clocks.

A thick mist enveloped Kathleen, permeating her skin, her flesh, her bones. A dizzy sensation raced through her, like the instant before losing consciousness, when vision slants and sounds become whispers. Her eyelids closed, and she was lulled into a state of utter relaxation, gently floating. Her body was weightless, riding on soft currents of air.

Though she couldn't actually see anything, images materialized in her mind. She saw an infant, kicking and laughing and waving a rattle. In her mind, she heard the wail of distant winds. And a child began to cry. There were flowers, the most fragrant bouquets. And the cries softened to the gentle whisper of a woman's laughter. She approached a coffin. Before she viewed the body, the lid closed with a resounding thud.

Then the winds faded to a breeze. It was dark. Very still. She was in the eye of a maelstrom.

Kathleen snapped awake. She was lying in her queen-size bed in her own condominium. The digital clock on the nightstand clicked to midnight.

She closed her eyes and opened them again. Was this really happening? This was certainly her bedroom. The cream-colored satin sheets belonged to her. There was the familiar scent of lavender potpourri. With a sort of wonderment, she picked up the magazine on her nightstand and read the date. June, one year ago. She had passed through some sort of time warp, gone back into the past.

Impossible! Such psychic events simply did not occur in reality. But that must be what had happened. The clock clicked to 12:01. She had one day, twenty-four hours, to live over again. And she mustn't waste a single moment.

She leapt from her bed and jumped into jeans and a T-shirt. Then she changed again. This was the most important day of her life, the day she would make Zachary Foster fall in love with her. She had to look wonderful. Where was that pearl gray silk blouse she'd bought last week?

Her walk-in closet was filled with clothing she'd owned a year ago. But of course! The other items hadn't been made yet. They didn't exist in this time.

But a glance in the mirror showed her that she had the chin-length haircut she'd gotten last week. Her makeup was the same as the makeup she'd worn to her office. But, physically, she wasn't the same woman she'd been one year ago. Nor emotionally. Kathleen had an additional year of growth and pain under her belt. The objects in her bedroom were from one year ago. But she'd changed.

This was magic! She ordered herself to take deep breaths. Her hand rested on her chest as if she could silence the pounding of her heart with a touch. She had a second chance. "Oh, gosh," she whispered, "I can't blow it!"

Her schedule for the next twenty-four hours must be planned with the strategy of a conquering general. She had to be sure that Foster would fall totally in love with her. That way he would understand her and all her fears. That way they wouldn't argue, and she wouldn't lash out at him. That way he would forgive anything.

One thing was very clear. Kathleen gulped down the panic that rose in her throat. She'd have to seduce him.

Today, she would take the first step from flirtation to eternal love. Today, they would join with a passion that must be strong enough to conquer time.

Today. Only one day. That was all the time she had.

Chapter Two

She had to plan. With an enormous, life-changing agenda ahead of her, Kathleen was overwhelmed. She started with the obvious: what to wear? She wanted to look sexy but not cheap. Stylish but not unapproachable.

Quickly sorting through her closet, Kathleen selected a short-sleeved turquoise cotton blouse tucked into black linen shorts. Her accessories were a silver concha belt, a silver-and-turquoise pendant and matching earrings. She splashed water on her face and reapplied her makeup. Kohl lined her dark brown eyes in a manner she hoped would make them flash flirtatiously. Her lipstick was coral but soft and enticing so that Foster wouldn't be able to resist tasting her lips.

"What am I doing?" She turned away from her reflection. Plotting his seduction, dressing herself like bait for a trap. How shallow!

She'd changed in the past year. Before her mother's stroke forced her to take on responsibility, she'd been blithe, lighthearted and more than a little bit spoiled. Her life philosophy could have been summed up in a few words: *Consequences? Who cares!*

But now, people depended upon her. Now, she knew the depths of sorrow, the dark side of her soul. And she suspected that manipulating Foster into bed wasn't fair, wasn't right. But her transaction with the time merchant had rewritten all the rules. She'd leapt back in time, hoping to make Zachary Foster fall in love with her and revise their tortured past, and she wasn't quite sure whether or not that was deceitful.

"Later," she promised herself. She'd think about ethics later. Right now, the clock was ticking. She had to take action or lose this chance forever.

She wore running shoes because she would have to move fast. But not too fast. She didn't want to frighten the poor man to death. As if that were possible! She couldn't imagine strong, manly Foster being afraid of anything.

Diving into the driver's seat of her bronze BMW sedan, she cautioned herself against speeding. Then again, if she got a traffic citation, what would happen? She couldn't appear for a court date in the year that had already occurred. Or could she? Would she? Had she already lived an alternative life?

The implications were staggering. She should have asked more questions of Diana Marie. For instance, at the end of the twenty-four hours, when Kathleen jumped forward in time, would she even remember what had happened? Would she recall the year to come—which was really the year that had already passed? She should have demanded something in writing.

Too late now.

She parked on the street in Foster's Capitol Hill neighborhood. In this older section of town, mature elms spread their branches in a high canopy above the street lamps. The night air felt fresh and pleasantly cool against her flushed skin.

Before her loomed a blond brick mansion that had been converted to apartments. Behind it was the refinished carriage house Foster used as his studio. Was he home? She trotted along the flagstone walk that circled the mansion.

His carriage house glowed like a jewel in the night. The curtains were open, and light poured from the skylights, as well. As she came closer, she heard the plaintive strains of a saxophone. Foster always played jazz tapes and CD's while he worked.

If she stood on tiptoe, she could peek inside his windows. Silently, she crept through the yard, past the shadowed rosebushes. Her fingertips touched the rough brick wall, and Kathleen froze like a statue. All too well, she remembered what she would find inside his studio. Even now, she didn't trust herself to face those portraits.

But should she peek inside to make sure he was alone?

No, she decided. She wouldn't start this precious day by spying on him.

She went back to the alley and tapped lightly on the door. "Foster, it's me. Kathleen."

He pulled open the door. He was shirtless and shoeless. His Levi's clung to his narrow hips and outlined his muscular thighs. His chest was lightly tanned and sprinkled with black hair much darker than the sun-streaked brown that fell across his forehead. She remembered the magnificent smell of oil paints and turpentine, a wonderful perfume. Her gaze focused on his welcoming smile, and happiness welled up within her. He was glad to see her.

His voice was husky, as if he hadn't spoken in hours. "Kind of late, Kathleen."

She didn't trust herself to respond. There were so many words to say, explanations and plans and promises. Where should she start?

"Kathleen?"

Moving in slow motion, as if in a dream, she glided toward him. Her arms twined around his neck. She went up on tiptoe and kissed him square on the mouth.

An indescribable pleasure shivered across her skin as her body pressed against his. When he held her and returned her kiss, her passion intensified until she was giddy. He cared for her! He could not hide it. Could not pretend otherwise. These feelings she was experiencing could not be wrong.

Dizzy with sweet relief, she looked up at him. The expression in his deep blue eyes was warm. "Oh, Foster. I've been wanting to do that for a year."

"But we've only known each other two months."

"Seems like a year," she said quickly, hoping to cover her mistake. She would have to be careful. "Doesn't it seem like we've known each other forever? For an eternity?"

"Eternity, huh?" He raised his eyebrows. "That's a hell of a long time."

"Hardly long enough." She walked her fingers up his bare chest, savoring their fond familiarity. He seemed so indulgent, so understanding. And she was tempted to level with him, to tell him that their relationship was so important that she'd come backward in time to put things right. "Do you believe in a time and space continuum?" she ventured.

For a moment, he looked baffled. "I haven't really given it much thought." Then he caught her hand, lifted it to his lips and turned it palm upward to kiss the soft, sensitive place at the base of her thumb. "I only focus on one thing at a time. Right now, I'm thinking of you."

"Are you? And what are you thinking about me?"

"I'm wondering why your eyes are so dark and mysterious tonight. You have a secret."

"Who, me? Not at all. I'm an open book."

"And there's something in your laughter."

Nervousness, he thought. Zach held her at arm's length and studied her graceful, symmetrical features in the glow from the porch light. Something about Kathleen was different, but he couldn't pinpoint what it was. Her posture? Her makeup? Her surprising kiss?

That had been one hell of a kiss. Even though he didn't make a practice of getting involved with his models or with clients who came to him for portraits, only a monk who took his vows of celibacy seriously could resist a woman as vivacious and ripe as Kathleen. After their second session, she'd given him a little kiss on the cheek. A few other times the startling, forbidden chemistry between them had come close to explosion. Still, he'd always managed to restrain himself before. But the kiss she'd just given him was different, more serious and a whole lot sexier. This kiss was hungry. And though he might be acting cool while he processed this new development, he was far from feeling cool.

"Your hair," he said. "You cut your hair."

"Do you like it?"

"It's pretty. You look old-fashioned, like a flapper."

"But I should have waited," she said guiltily, "until you were done with my portrait. That was the first thing you told me when I came to you for a sitting. Don't change anything."

"It's no problem. I'm almost done with the paintings."

"But I feel terrible. You specifically told me—"

"It's okay." He had liked her thick mane of untamed black hair, but this new look intrigued him. He turned her head sideways to study her profile. The bob emphasized the straight line of her jaw and her sculpted cheekbones. He held her chin and turned her face toward him again. "The haircut shows off your eyes to perfection."

"Do I inspire you?"

"Absolutely." More than she knew. And, because of who she was, that attraction was more dangerous than dynamite. She'd gotten inside his head and haunted his dreams. He couldn't stop thinking about her, couldn't stop painting her. Variations on her eyes. On the arch of her throat. The straight line of her backbone. Her hips. Her thighs. "Come on inside. I've got something to show you."

Not yet, she prayed.

"I want you to see the paintings I'm going to display at Kendall Gallery. My showing is the day after tomorrow."

When he grasped her hand and pulled her toward the open door, she balked. "Actually," she said, "I— I want you to come with me."

"Where?"

She seemed flustered. When her gaze slid away from his, he knew she was being evasive. Lying to him. Why?

She stammered when she said, "It's . . . it's the hair thing."

"What's going on, Kathleen? What are you up to?"

"Nothing!" she protested.

He didn't believe that for one minute. Whenever a woman said "nothing," it meant something. But what?

"About my hair," she continued. "As soon as I got it whacked off, I thought about all the work you've done on my portrait. And I realized that I'd ruined everything. I couldn't sleep."

"It's really not a big deal. We can work around it."

"But I have a solution. We can go down to Welles and pick out a wig."

"Right now?"

"After midnight is the perfect time to shop. There are so few customers crowding the aisles."

Though her lovely eyes blinked wide and guileless, he still suspected a hidden motive. "Tell me what you want, Kathleen. I don't like being manipulated."

"Manipulated?" There was the nervous laugh again. "I would never—"

"Sure you would. What's going on? What are the rules of this game?"

"It's no game." Her tone was serious. "My future and yours depend upon . . . I can't explain."

"Then I'll have to guess."

It shouldn't be too hard to figure out what she was hiding. He'd spent hours painting her and was keenly attuned to her moods. He'd seen her when she was pensive. Excited. Dreamy and relaxed, with her eyelids half-closed. He knew the difference between her polite laughter and genuine amusement. A flash of her notorious temper could stiffen her entire body.

Right now, he sensed an intensity in her. A desperation. And a heat. My God, she was hot. The warmth that radiated from her shot straight to his heart.

To his heart? Zach almost laughed at that high-minded sentiment. Surely the beautiful Kathleen Welles simply aroused a different part of his anatomy.

"Please, Foster. You've got to come with me."

She stuck her fists on her hips, and her breasts jutted. His gaze followed the angle of her elbow, the flare of her hips, the balanced curves of her shapely legs. And he realized there wasn't much he could refuse her.

"Please," she repeated. "I thought artists were supposed to be spontaneous."

"Don't tease me, Kathleen. You might be playing with fire."

"Really?" Even her voice sizzled. "And will I get burned?"

He caught her around the waist and pulled her against him, arching her back. With his other hand, he stroked her chin, her throat, her collarbone. Finally, he held the firm roundness of one breast. Beneath her brassiere, the nipple was a tight nub.

He lifted her slightly, and her pelvis rubbed against his. Though her expression was startled, he heard the need in her gasp, saw it in her eyes.

"Foster, wait." Her hands were braced against his bare chest, half pushing him away, half caressing. "Not here. Not yet."

"You started this fire," he growled.

"But I didn't expect a four-alarm blaze." She wrenched away from him. "Besides, we're putting on quite a show for your neighbors."

"Then come inside," he urged.

"Absolutely not." This was very important. Making love would change both their lives. The timing had to be exactly right.

"Please trust me," she said. "I know what I'm doing." She hoped she did.

Driving him crazy—that was what she was doing. He took a step away from her. "Maybe we should say good-night, Kathleen."

"Wait. Don't go. I—I don't want to be away from you."

Zach nearly groaned aloud. First she kissed him, then she pushed him away, then she wanted him again. What was he? A yo-yo? "Which is it?"

"Come with me."

Despite his annoyance, there was something compelling in her voice, a persuasive note that he could not ignore. With a long-suffering sigh, he stepped into his studio, grabbed a shirt and stuck his bare feet into loafers. "Okay. Let's go."

The Denver streets seemed nearly deserted after midnight. Foster leaned back in the passenger seat of Kathleen's BMW and absorbed the quiet darkness he loved. In New York and even San Francisco, there was unceasing action, a constant energy that overloaded his senses and crowded his paintings. But here he could appreciate the stillness that seemed to flow from the mountains and touch the people who lived in their shadow. He'd grown up in Colorado, and he always thought of Denver as home.

With its sweeping, craggy panoramas, this land was an artist's paradise. But Zach found that he preferred to catch the reflection of a mountain sunset in the eyes of a beautiful woman. Portraits were his first love. The series of paintings using Kathleen Welles as a model represented the best work he'd done in his life. He was eager to hear the critical reaction at the gallery on Friday.

He glanced toward her, wishing he could paint her with her new hairdo. It was a major change in her appearance, as if she'd been transformed overnight from a frivolous girl to a very provocative woman. Maybe he'd have time for a sketch or two, even a quick acrylic.

"You've changed, Kathleen. And it's not just the haircut. Tell me why."

She shrugged, looking nervous, worried, as if, he thought, she carried a heavy weight on those slender shoulders.

"Did something bad happen?" he asked.

"Very much the contrary." At a stoplight, she tossed her head and seemed to confront him, almost challenge him. "I believe everything will turn out for the good."

"Whatever you say, princess."

"Princess," she repeated softly. "Why do you call me that?"

"You remind me of the stories my grandmother sometimes read to me and my brothers before we went to sleep. The princesses were always very beautiful."

"I like that."

"And they always made these weird demands before they would get involved with a guy."

"Such as?" she asked.

"You know the drill," he said. "Bring me the moon and the stars. Slay the dragon. Climb a glass mountain. Bring me a lock of hair from the ogre."

She nodded. "That must be why I liked those stories."

"Those princesses were willful, stubborn and demanding. And selfish. Like you."

Her eyebrows raised. "Selfish?"

"In the best sense of the word," he said diplomatically. "Your selfishness is unconscious, like a force of nature. The ocean reclaiming the shore. The sunrise demanding that the night make way."

"Charming comparison, Foster."

"The first time we met, you were giving orders," he reminded her. "You came marching into the window display and tore a mauve scarf off a mannequin's throat because you wanted to wear that scrap of silk yourself."

"You agreed with me," she said. "You said the scarf looked better on me than on a plastic statue. I gave it life. That's what you said."

Foster remembered. And though the truth had sounded like a corny line, it had worked. Within a matter of moments, he'd made an appointment with a classy woman who'd never associated with a window designer in her life. The lovely heiress, Kathleen Welles. She was spirited, brash, demanding...and, yes, selfish. Immediately, he had wanted to capture her on canvas.

She swerved her BMW into the parking lot across the street from Welles and flung open her car door.

"What's the hurry?" he asked.

"Time is incredibly important. Every minute, every second, should be lived to the fullest."

That didn't sound like the Kathleen he'd come to know over the past couple of months. She was chronically late, irresponsible in a way that could be infuriating. But here she was, rushing him across the deserted downtown Denver street to repair a mistake she felt she'd made by getting her hair cut.

He climbed out of the car and checked the time on his pocket watch. "Twelve forty-seven," he said.

"What's that?"

He showed her the small silver pocket watch resting in the center of his hand. "Belonged to my grandmother. She wore it as a locket." He closed the engraved lid. "Those are her initials. B.A.F. Beatrice Anne Foster."

"And you carry her watch as a remembrance."

"I guess so. Besides, I don't like to wear anything on my wrist when I paint."

They crossed the street, and at the store's rear door Kathleen buzzed for the night watchman. Half to herself, she said, "We really ought to update this security system."

"Has there ever been a break-in?"

"Once there was. We had a jewelry display in one of the small side windows." She glanced up at him sharply, recalling the argument they'd just had about using real diamonds. Of course, he wouldn't remember...because it hadn't happened yet. "The thief was caught when he tried to fence the gems."

"Then no real harm was done."

"But it could have been awful. We could have lost thousands of dollars' worth of jewelry."

"*We?*" he questioned. "I've never heard you refer to Welles as *we* before."

That was because she hadn't been president before. In real time, one year from now, she'd learned to take her responsibilities seriously. But that was the future. As far as Foster was concerned, Kathleen still held the position of buyer, a job that was hectic during the spring and fall fashion showings in New York and Europe. After she made selections, she pretty much coasted through the rest of the year, passing on her more mundane duties to an assistant.

The watchman showed his sleepy face at the door and let them inside. He didn't seem terribly surprised to see her. "Working late, Miss Welles?"

"Actually, we're just browsing."

"I'll leave the keys in the door so's you can leave whenever you're ready. Okay?"

Actually, to the new Kathleen, leaving the keys for her convenience seemed a ridiculous breach of the minimal security, but she couldn't chastise the guard just now. "Thank you."

Setting out with long strides, she waved to Foster. "Come on, this way."

There were only a few security lights around the perimeter of the first floor, but darkness was no obstacle for her. Kathleen knew the layout of the store as well as she knew the furniture in her own condo. She'd grown up in this store. When she was a little girl and her father was still alive, he would bring her to Welles and show her how everything worked. They operated the elevators and checked the inventory. He'd always found something for them to repair or improve—a wobbly rack, an inconvenient display, a cracked tile. Her mother, however, had run Welles single-handedly during the ten years since her father passed away.

"Wait up," Zach called after her. "I can't see where I'm going."

"Sorry."

When she stood still in the darkness, Kathleen suddenly sensed her father's presence. Though she couldn't gaze directly into his face, he seemed to be somewhere just beyond her range of vision. Was he here, perhaps existing in a time bubble of his own?

For a moment, she almost wished she'd bought a different day from Diana Marie Casey. Her eighth birthday.

And with that thought, she saw the day quite clearly. In her memory? In reality? Her father had given her a bicycle, and they'd spent the entire day together in the park while he taught her how to ride.

Sudden tears stung the backs of her eyelids, but she rapidly blinked them away. There wasn't time for regrets and remembrance. She'd spent the past year torturing herself with second guesses. And now she had her chance to make a difference. She must not let it slip away.

"Kathleen?" Zachary came up beside her. "Are you all right?"

"I was thinking about my father."

"Was he the founder of Welles?"

"No, his grandfather was. This department store has been around for more than eighty years. We've gone from corsets and garters to panty hose and lacy teddies." Time, she thought, changed everything. "I wish you could have known my father. In his own way, he was an artist. You would have liked him."

And her father would have liked Zach Foster. He would have appreciated this strong man who could balance his daughter's whimsies. He would have approved of the fact that Foster kept himself gainfully employed while he pursued his dream of a career in art.

Her mother, on the other hand, decidedly did not approve of Kathleen forming an attachment to a window dresser. Hannah Welles tried to run her daughter's life with the same demanding efficiency that she brought to the department store.

"This is really my mother's store now," she said. "After my father died, Hannah put her whole life into Welles."

"She's done a good job."

"But this is all she lives for. Foster, she's down here all the time. Sometimes she comes in at six in the morning and stays until midnight." That kind of work wasn't healthy. Kathleen knew from her year as president that the store could absorb every waking moment if you let it. And with the clarity of hindsight, she saw that perhaps it was inevitable that, without balance in her life, her mother would finally collapse under the pressure.

"Let's go," she said. She held out her hand, and when Foster clasped her outstretched fingers, she felt a firm and solid contact, a fulfillment.

For a moment, they stood beside a perfume counter, and the heady fragrances teased Kathleen's nostrils, stimulated all her senses. It seemed she had never before experienced things so vividly. Perhaps everything was better the second time around?

"Where are you leading me?" Foster asked.

"Second floor. Near the beauty salon."

They climbed the unmoving escalator. The second floor was even darker than the first. The only illumination came from a couple of security lamps and the diffuse flow of moonlight through the tall windows. Yet Foster now moved smoothly with her toward the small display of wigs. *Graceful* was too pretty a word for a man masculine enough for Helen to call a thug, but Kathleen had never seen him take a misstep. It was as if he always knew exactly where he was going and how to get there. So unlike her—and one of the many things she admired about him.

She found a light switch behind the counter area and flicked it on. They were bathed in a circle of light that shone on an array of real and synthetic hair.

And Zachary Foster seemed suddenly rapt with the possibilities for artistic experimentation. He indicated a long silvery blond wig. "Try this one on."

"Foster, I am not a Barbie doll."

He lifted the wig off a faceless plastic head. "Sit down, Kathleen. I'm the artist here. Your job is to sit quietly."

Grumbling, she perched on a high stool opposite a mirror. Her fingers laced tightly together while he approached her with the wig. Leaving fashion decisions to someone else made her nervous in the extreme. Kathleen had been born with a sense of style, perhaps a genetic gift from a mother who was always beautifully groomed, accessorized and color coordinated. Both she and Hannah hated to leave home looking less than perfect.

Indeed, after Hannah's stroke, her first conscious thought pertained to wardrobe. Though she could barely move and her memory had gone on the fritz, she couldn't endure being seen in a hospital-issue gown, and Kathleen had had to personally select the nighties and robes for her mother's stay at Mercy Hospital.

"Close your eyes," Foster ordered.

Uncharacteristically, Kathleen obeyed.

Early this morning, she remembered, she would see her mother, because that was what she had done before. This time, however, they would not argue.

This time, Kathleen was determined to convince her mother to see a doctor for a checkup. Not her regular physician, but a specialist. Kathleen would arrange for her mother to see Dr. Gregory Mathers, the specialist who had been treating her for the past year. Surely he would find the signs of her impending stroke. She would be treated and spared a year of agony. That turn of events would make this journey in time worth the effort, even if things didn't work out with Foster.

He'd finished arranging her wig, and she felt his hands at her throat, adjusting the collar of her turquoise blouse. "What are you doing?"

"Completing the look."

"May I see?"

"Sure."

Kathleen opened her eyes. The silver-blond wig was startling, especially since Foster had turned the collar of her turquoise blouse up and widened the neckline to show cleavage. She looked like a different woman entirely, and the effect was unsettling.

"Interesting, but it's not right," Foster observed. "Close your eyes again. I want to try something else."

She lowered her eyelids but peeked through her lashes, secretly watching him as he selected another wig. Perhaps because Foster worked as a window dresser and had an artist's objectivity, he brought none of the typical masculine discomfort to handling feminine accessories. And his deft, masterful maneuverings of them made him seem even more manly, if such a thing were possible.

Kathleen gulped and tried to ask casually, "So, how did you get started as a window designer?"

"I was in New York, studying art, dead broke as usual. One of the other students told me about a window-dressing job with a guy who was an off-Broadway set designer." She felt him arrange the wig on her head. "I showed up. He told me the theme was circus. I made up some of the mannequins faces as clowns, and I experimented with zebra and tiger stripes on the others. Everyone raved about the bold, new 'savage' look, and the rest, as they say, is history."

"Do you like the work?"

"Let's just say there isn't a hell of a lot of gainful employment for artists." His hands rested on her shoulders. "Open your eyes."

Her reflection in the mirror showed a sophisticated, cool, dark-eyed redhead. "Not bad," she murmured. "But this isn't helping us find a wig I can wear for sittings."

He twirled her around on the stool to face him. "I told you to forget about that. I have. And I'm done here. Wouldn't you like to go back to my studio now and see yourself on canvas?"

No, she silently vowed. Not yet. She wasn't ready. Lightly, she deflected his invitation. "Are you inviting me to your place to show me your etchings? Really, Foster. Do you think I'll fall for a line as antiquated as that one?"

Briefly matching her lightness, he said, "Well, we could move on to designer sheets and find a king-size bed."

She vacillated between desire and prudence. When they made love, it had to be more than sex. It must be forever. The moment had to be so perfect that any wounds she'd inflicted last year would heal and he would forgive her anything. He must not only make love to her; he must love her.

This was so difficult. She removed the auburn wig and smoothed her own black hair. Looking up, she saw him watching her.

"You're different," he said once more. "More serious. More..." He paused. "When are you going to tell me the cause of this interesting transformation?"

She stared directly into the inviting azure of his gaze. Did she dare to tell him the truth? Did she dare not to? What sort of relationship would they have if she wasn't honest with him?

Chapter Three

Conflicting goals warred within her. She needed to be honest. But she also wanted to entice Foster, to make him look upon her as a fascinating, desirable woman, not a wacko who believed in time travel.

"Tell me what's happened."

She couldn't tell him. Not yet. She couldn't take the chance that he'd be angry or wouldn't believe her. She paced away from him, thinking, considering. Here, in the Welles department store, she was in her element. Here, perhaps, she could find the tools she needed to make him fall in love.

"First," she said, "I have a request."

He watched her, his expression wary.

"I'm going to want another portrait," she improvised. "A gift for my mother."

"Any of the three I've already done would be perfect."

"Foster!" She glared at him. "I can't give my mother one of those."

"Why not?"

Because she was nude. But she couldn't say that, because he didn't know that she'd seen the paintings. God, this was complicated. Remembering the future and balancing the past. "I need something totally sophisticated for Hannah," she explained. "I'd need to be dressed in a designer original and accessorized to within an inch of my life. Are the paintings you've finished appropriate?"

He was silent.

She confronted him. "Well, are they?"

It suddenly occurred to her that she wasn't the only one harboring a deception. He *knew* she'd be upset at a public display of her nudity.

She nearly groaned. Zach Foster might be a gifted artist, but Hannah was right about one thing. He didn't have the slightest regard for social propriety. However, the time was not right for this debate. "Come with me. We're going to find clothes for my next portrait."

"Hold it!" He checked his grandmother's silver watch again. "It's almost one-fifteen, Kathleen. I'm going to need some sleep. I have to get ready for the showing."

"You can sleep tomorrow." Today, she thought, is mine.

Taking his hand, she guided him through the dim light to the unmoving escalator. They climbed carefully to the third floor, where the designer clothing was discreetly displayed for those customers who could afford the pricey boutique. Every item was one of a kind. An original.

"Very classy," Foster said when he sauntered through the glass doors into the posh area decorated in Queen Anne style with a crystal chandelier overhead. "Everything but a harpist, caviar and champagne," he said.

"There is a small fridge," she said. "Why don't you get us some refreshments?"

"Point me toward it."

He left her, and Kathleen pondered the ornate beaded dresses, the subtle silks and the imported creations. On one rack, all by itself, a bridal gown gleamed through the plastic protecting the satin and lace of the purest white.

She smiled wryly. A vision of her in that dress would doubtless send a man like Zach Foster screaming into the night.

Still, she needed an outfit that would create an unforgettable impression in his mind. She found a fabulous cocktail dress in a soft, heavy silk, the bright scarlet devilishly right for her complexion.

She heard the pop of a cork and turned.

"I like the way rich people live." In one hand, Foster held an opened bottle of champagne, in the other, two fluted crystal glasses. He poured. "Shopping with champagne. Now that's civilized."

He sprawled on a blue velvet love seat. But before she could disappear into the dressing room, he caught her hand. "You know, Kathleen, it's late. I don't need a fashion show right now."

"Yes, you do." Fashion was her best skill, and she wanted to impress him.

She slipped into the dressing room and the silk confection. She regarded her reflection in the full-length mirror. Rubies would be the perfect complement, but she suspected Foster would be too impatient if she ran down to the ground floor and pawed through the selection of jewelry. Simplicity would have to suffice.

Barefoot in a designer frock, she looked sophisticated but womanly. Rich, but not unreachable. With luck, any man with half a libido could fall in love with her. It was time to make her entrance.

She stepped into the glow of a spotlight in the area where Foster was sitting. In her work as a buyer, Kathleen had had the opportunity to observe the most exclusive fashion models in the world, and now she copied their moves, lightly swishing the fabric, twirling on her toes, posing for him.

"Could you paint me like this? Would you?" she asked breathlessly.

"I would, if you want. But I've already captured the spirit of who you are. And it doesn't have a damn thing to do with what you're wearing."

"Foster, don't be naive. Clothing creates an impression. Style has a great deal to do with what we think of people."

"Maybe for you," he said.

"Oh?"

"When I look at you, Kathleen, I see a woman who is bright and witty and impulsive." He held out a glass of champagne to her.

She accepted and took a sip.

He continued. "I see a free spirit. And right now, I see that something is bothering you. Come here." He patted the space beside him on the love seat.

When she sat, he watched every nuance of her expression. His curiosity made her feel oddly exposed.

"Okay, Kathleen. No more evasion. Tell me what's going on."

She gulped her champagne. The truth? "I went to a . . . a time merchant."

"Oh, well, that explains everything." She saw the sardonic lift of his eyebrows. "A fortune-teller?"

"Not exactly. She didn't tell me the future." Because Kathleen already knew what would happen in the future.

"Then she traffics in karma and past-life regressions? That sort of thing?"

"In a way." How could she explain? She'd lived a year, regretting that she'd lost him. She had the perspective of the future. In the past. "It's complicated," she muttered.

"Uh-huh." He filled their glasses again. "Try to explain. And the simple truth would be best. Why are you different today than you were yesterday?"

"There's nothing simple about the truth." Because she hadn't known how deeply she loved him until she'd lost him. She hadn't recognized the depth of her thirst until the well was dry. "All I can tell you is that the events of these twenty-four hours, from midnight to midnight, are incredibly important."

"Why?"

His expression showed a healthy skepticism, and she realized that probably she would have exactly the same reaction to someone who believed in such magic. It was sheer, unbelievable nonsense. And yet, here she was, reliving a day in her past.

As she gazed at him, she melted inside. He was so perfect, the man of her dreams. From his unruly brown hair to the frayed cuffs of his Levi's, Zachary Emile Foster was everything she ever wanted in a man. "What would you say if I told you this was the last day we would be... together?"

"I'd say that's up to us," he scoffed. "Come on, Kathleen. You can't be serious about believing some hocus-pocus from some charlatan. They'll say anything if you cross their palms with enough silver. How much did you pay her?"

"Enough." Seventy-five thousand dollars' worth of enough.

"And what did you get for your money? Some kind of magical charm or potion?"

"Time," she said. "I bought time from her. No promises. No guarantees. The rest is up to me."

"Time. That's interesting," he mused. "Buying time but not promises sounds like an actual bit of wisdom, not the usual junk from a fortune-teller with a dime-store Ouija board and a couple of crystals. It also sounds like life. Time is the gift we all have when we start out."

"But sometimes we misuse time."

"Wasted youth? Hell yes, at the ripe old age of thirty-three, even I can go along with that."

Zach rubbed his chin thoughtfully. When he'd dropped out of high school, he'd messed up worse than six sides of dammit. In and out of trouble, he'd been arrested for shoplifting. Had lost his driver's license after five speeding tickets. Et cetera. It was a miracle that he'd survived.

"I'm only twenty-six—uh, twenty-five—and I have regrets, too," Kathleen offered.

He glanced at her, and the depth of her gaze held his attention. Though Kathleen was too well-bred to bite her fingernails or fidget, she was obviously distressed. After spending these weeks with her, he could read her emotions well.

Zach tried to take her encounter with the occultist seriously, but he'd known too many gullible people who got swept away with such fantasies. And life had made him a realist.

"Okay, princess," he said. "I'll give you the benefit of the doubt. What did the time merchant tell you? Why won't we be together at the end of the day?"

"We're going to hurt each other." She cast her eyes downward, and he saw the beginnings of tears. A flash of temper and tears wouldn't have surprised him yesterday. But now, her sorrow felt oddly heavy, almost tangible.

Protectively, he wrapped her in his arms. When she leaned against him, her body felt as delicate and vulnerable as a wounded sparrow. "I won't hurt you. I promise. And I won't let anyone else hurt you, either." Damn that occult fraud, wherever she was. He stroked Kathleen's silken hair. "Hush now, you're safe with me. Don't cry."

She sat up and dashed away her tears. With visible effort, she pulled herself together. "You're absolutely right, Foster. I mustn't waste time crying." She smoothed her skirt, straightened her shoulders. "There's so much to be done. Besides, I don't want to ruin this dress. This bit of fabric costs over four thousand dollars. It wouldn't do to have it splotched with tears, would it?"

He shook his head, pleased that she'd overcome whatever had caused her emotional crisis but still curious. It did not escape his attention that she hadn't really told him anything yet. "You get changed, Kathleen. We're both tired. We need some sleep. We'll talk about this tomorrow."

She hurried into the dressing room and returned quickly. "I have one more thing to show you before we leave the store."

He sighed. "Lead on."

Once again, she directed him higher. They ended on the top floor. She pointed to a staircase. "This is a special place, Foster."

He nodded. This was another characteristic of those fairy-tale princesses; they always seemed to have access to enchanted places hidden from mere mortals.

Their footfalls echoed in the concrete stairwell that stretched to a bright red door marked Roof.

Kathleen went up on tiptoe and took a key from the ledge above the door. "My father used to work long hours, and he needed an escape that was closer than home. This was like a secret clubhouse to me when I was a kid."

She unfastened the lock and twisted the knob. "My mom comes here, too, when she's really tired. But we're the only ones who know about what's up here."

He followed her to her magical kingdom. Eight stories high, they could see the city lights sparkle around them. In the blue glow of moonlight, Zach could see the shadows of distant mountains to the west. Overhead were galaxies. Beside him, Kathleen seemed to emit her own special illumination. A soft, magical glow.

"Do you like it?" she asked.

"It's an amazing view."

"There's more. Come over here."

In the center of the roof was a square structure no more than ten feet high. Kathleen found a door that was invisible to Foster in the dim light, and she pushed it open.

Inside was a tiny apartment. A closet bathroom, a wet bar, a bed and a rolltop desk spilling over with ledgers and notes. The colors were dark, cool and cozy. "This is great," he said. "It's like an urban cave."

Kathleen laughed with delight, and her pleasure penetrated to the inner core of him.

"I always thought it was more like a nest, an eagle's aerie," she said. "My parents used to spend a lot of time here."

At the desk, amid the notes her mother was working on, she found a pewter-framed photo of her parents. Black-and-white, it was an artistic shot of Hannah gazing up into Jonah Welles's eyes. She showed it to Foster.

"I can see your features in both of them. You don't have brothers or sisters, do you?"

"I had a brother. When I was sixteen, he was killed in the car accident with my father."

"I'm sorry."

"Me, too."

Yet Kathleen felt that her dark sadness was a mere sliver compared to Hannah's agony. On the day she lost both husband and son, all the light went out of her life. "My brother was driving. He was only twenty. They'd gone on a camping trip in the mountains. The two Welles men, doing manly bonding. But they never came back."

She sighed. "Things would have been so different if they were around."

Her mother might not have made the store into her whole life. If there had been other family, Hannah might not have immersed herself so obsessively in every aspect of the adult Kathleen's existence. And then, Kathleen thought sadly, Hannah wouldn't have been so disappointed in her daughter.

"It's after two o'clock," Foster said gently. "I've been working around the clock to get ready for the opening. Kathleen, I need some sleep."

She gestured to the bed. "Make yourself comfortable."

Though eyeing her quizzically, he did so, lying on his back with his long legs stretched out. He kicked the loafers off his sockless feet. "Are you going to join me?" He offered a tired but sexy smile.

"Oh, Foster!" she protested prettily. It was so tempting. But not yet. She stayed at the desk, not trusting herself to come closer to him. When they made love, she wanted it to be perfect. There were too many ghosts in this place. She wouldn't feel as if they were alone.

Foster closed his eyes. In moments, his breathing was slow and steady. He worked long hours, pushing himself physically, she thought. That was why he could fall asleep so quickly. To Kathleen, slumber never came easily.

She crept to the bedside and sat beside him, studying the planes of his face. Even in repose, he looked ready for action. His jaw was tense. The frown lines between his eyebrows did not relax. But his lips, slightly parted, were an invitation to a kiss.

If she really were a princess, she might take advantage of his sleep, kiss him and bind him to her forever. If only she had access to that brand of magic.

She reached across to the bedside table where he'd placed his silver pocket watch. Two hours of her precious day had been spent. There were other plans to be made, other strategies, but she was exhausted, too.

Kathleen stretched out beside him and rested her eyes. But her mind was not still. She drifted immediately from worries to a dream filled with ticking clocks and hourglasses. She heard the voice of Diana Marie, taunting her. "You're seeking the impossible, princess. There's no such thing as love eternal."

"There is," Kathleen protested. More dream images flitted across her mind. She ordered herself to awaken but could not. Then she saw an image of Foster coming toward her. He wore his usual Levi's, but the broad expanse of his chest was covered by armor. Light shone from his blue eyes. "I seek the truth," he said.

"No!" Why not? What was she so afraid of? To his dream image, she said, "If you knew how terrible I had been the first time I lived this day, you would never forgive me."

"Very well, my princess." He knelt before her. "I seek your hand."

Kathleen extended her palm and noticed her ornate sleeve. She was clad in fine gold brocade. Princess wear, she thought. She touched the top of her head and felt the spikes of a jeweled tiara.

"I have killed the dragon," he said. "As proof, I bring you the bloody jewel from the center of his forehead."

Triumphantly, he held aloft a shining green stone, slick with blood. "For you, Princess."

Not knowing what else to say, Kathleen nodded. "Very nice."

"But that is not all, Your Highness. I have caught the sacred toad."

"Nice," Kathleen repeated, staring at a huge, slimy frog. This fairy-tale-princess business wasn't all it was cracked up to be. "Put it over there, if you don't mind."

"And the magical cockroach."

A shudder of pure revulsion went through her. "Over there."

"Last but not least," he said, "the head of the witch."

He held the gruesome thing by the hair, and Kathleen saw the face of Diana Marie, disembodied, still laughing and shrieking, "Eternal love! It's a lie! A lie!"

Kathleen covered her face with her hands. Blindly, she ran away from the vision. Only a dream. She was only dreaming. But she entered a sticky mire that clung to her brocaded gown and weighed her down until she could not move.

Her eyes flew open, and she saw Foster gazing down at her. The first words from her mouth were "The time! What time is it?"

"A little after seven."

Panic made her alert. "I've wasted five hours! There's so much to do!"

"Slow down, Kathleen."

"I can't. Foster, you don't understand!" Twenty-four hours minus seven was seventeen. Only seventeen hours to save her mother from a stroke and to establish the foundations for eternal love. How could she do it? How could she not?

"Relax," he advised. "No matter what you have to do today, it'll all be here tomorrow. *Mañana*."

"But it won't!" she said.

"Is this that mystical stuff again?" he demanded.

"I can't explain." She bolted from the bed and into the tiny closet of a bathroom, where she brushed her teeth and washed off the dregs of her makeup. She was a mess, an absolute mess. How could she possibly hope to seduce him eternally when she looked so utterly ghastly?

Making the best of her appearance, she returned to the bedside. The light cover was askew. But Foster was gone. It took no more than a glance to see every corner of this cozy hideaway. He'd left. Kathleen's heart sank. Had she driven him away with her inane story?

Her panic redoubled. This perfect seduction was going to be harder than she imagined. But she braced herself. She would convince him to give her another chance. She would make him love her, even if it took a magic toad and a sacred cockroach to do it.

Foster pushed open the door from outside and sauntered toward her as if nothing were wrong. "Come on, Kathleen. The morning view of the mountains is unbelievable. Too bad we slept through the sunrise."

Relief overwhelmed her, and she flung herself into his arms, ignoring caution and planning and clever scheme. She wanted to be with him, to love him. And she couldn't wait.

He responded immediately, holding her close, kissing her on the lips. They grappled with each other, clinging, craving, seeking to assuage an insatiable thirst.

She felt his hands on her breasts, his fingers fumbling with the buttons on her shirt. His mouth was hard against hers. His tongue penetrated her lips. She clawed at his back, his torso, the muscles in his thighs. She sought his hard arousal.

Kathleen could have asked him to stop. He would, she knew, if she objected. But she could not hold herself back. This was what she wanted, wasn't it? This was what she had longed for during the year when they were apart. Oh, God, she could not stop.

Then she heard a click, the sound of the door opening, a woman's voice. Her mother's voice.

"What's going on here?" Hannah Welles demanded. "Kathleen!"

Kathleen tore herself away from Foster, confused and pawing at her disheveled clothing. This was not supposed to be happening. "Mother?"

"I am terribly disappointed in you, Kathleen. Not surprised, but—"

"Why are you here?" The last time Kathleen had lived this day, her mother had awakened with a headache and had not arisen at her customary hour.

"I couldn't sleep." Hannah turned stiffly on her heel. "I will see you in my office, young lady. And you, Mr. Foster, obviously don't comprehend the duties of a window dresser. Please keep your hands off the merchandise."

He chuckled softly, not in the least bit intimidated by Hannah's outrage. "All I've stolen is a kiss. And I won't give that back."

Hannah stormed away, her step crisp, her bearing almost military.

Kathleen fell back on the bed. "This couldn't possibly be worse."

He sat beside her. "Come on, Kathleen, it's not that bad. You're twenty-five. Surely, your mother is aware that you haven't been living in a glass case, untouched and untouchable."

"You don't understand," she said. "My mother is ill. It's not healthy for her to be upset. I was hoping to convince her to go to the doctor today."

"Is it serious?"

"Very. She's on the verge of a stroke."

And Kathleen had to change that event. Or else, at fifteen minutes past four o'clock this afternoon, her mother would suffer a stroke that would incapacitate her for a year.

Chapter Four

"But it's not your problem, Foster." She stepped onto the rooftop, sucked down a breath of cool morning air and looked to the mountains for strength. "I'll take care of this situation with my mother. I'll talk to her."

"I'll go with you."

"Not necessary." And not prudent, Kathleen thought. The first time she and her mother had argued, a year ago in real time, the major cause of their disagreement was Foster. Though Kathleen had ached for him for one full year, having him standing beside her now, playing the role of her lover, might send her mother into a fit of absolute fury, bringing on her stroke.

Oblivious to her secret concerns, Foster stood beside her, gazing toward the west. "It's beautiful, the way the fog from the mountains seems to dissipate into a mirage of summer heat."

It was a beautiful thing to say. Artistic. Perceptive.

"Now let's go see your mother," he added.

Unrealistic. Stubborn. Bullheaded, she thought, contrasting her prior opinion. "Are you looking for a fight?"

"I've never run from one. But that's not what this is about. Last night, I said I wouldn't let anyone hurt you. I meant it. Not even Hannah."

"I know you mean well." A few minutes earlier, she'd been devastated when she thought he'd left. Now she was devastated that he wanted to stay by her side and protect her like some misguided knight-errant. "But I'd prefer to handle this by myself. I really can't allow my mother to be upset."

"Kathleen, are you so very concerned about what your mother thinks? Or anybody else, for that matter?"

Was he challenging her, Kathleen wondered. "Usually, I'm not." Not anymore. "But today is... different. There's something I need to do for my mother. And it has to be today. And I don't want to fight with her."

He began to pace. "I've seen you blow off a whole day of work to hang out in my studio," he observed.

"You're right." Or, he was, once.

"You come in late and leave early."

"Right again."

He circled behind her where she stood with her back to the sun. "You don't act like someone who gives a damn about anyone else's concerns."

Chagrined, she remembered all too well. *Irresponsible* would have been a kind description for her behavior. "I must be a classic case of arrested development. Still acting out a rebellious phase that has lasted much too long."

"Do you even care about your work?"

"I could." She paused for a moment, balancing past, present and future. "I will love my work. There's great satisfaction in doing a job well, behaving like an adult."

He stopped his pacing, his eyes comically wide, his expression a caricature of disbelief. He stepped straight up to her. "Excuse me? Did the princess say she liked behaving like an adult?"

"Okay," she allowed, "maybe I've acted like a spoiled brat."

He cupped his ear as if he were hard-of-hearing. "Maybe?"

"Don't push it, Foster. I've changed. People do change, you know. And that's one of the reasons I have to talk with Hannah. Alone."

Kathleen knew exactly what she must do: avoid a stressful confrontation with her mother and somehow convince Hannah to go to the doctor. With her mother's physical problems under control, she could concentrate on her relationship with Foster. "Will you be in your studio later?"

"Most of the day. I have a few more paintings to wrap and cart over to Kendall Gallery. One of my assistants, Donny, is taking care of windows today."

"I'll catch up with you," she promised. She reached up tentatively and caressed his cheek, half expecting him to pull away from her, to make a joke. Instead, he caught her hand and held it to his lips. "Oh, Foster," she whispered, "I'm going to hate being apart. Even if it's only for an hour. But I need to talk with my mother."

"I know you do. And I'm coming with you."

"Not a good plan," she said, gently reclaiming her hand. "If it's your job that you're worried about—"

"My job? Hell, Kathleen, I couldn't care less about that. Welles is my biggest account but not my only account. I have a waiting list of people who want me to work for them. There's a mall in Littleton that's offering me three times what I make at Welles."

"Really?"

"You don't have to sound so amazed," he said. "It's not exactly a vote of confidence."

"It's not that. Your work is excellent. Unbelievably good. I just can't believe that you've stayed with Welles . . . under the circumstances." Oops. Again she had to juggle past and future, what had and hadn't yet happened. During the year after their argument, he'd resented her so thoroughly that they'd almost never talked. "If you have more lucrative offers, why do you stay here?"

"I like the space. There aren't many department stores left in Denver, and Welles has a large display area. I can be creative here."

"But if the money is better—"

"I don't care about money."

"Foster, everybody cares about money."

He laughed. "Well, I don't. There are other considerations for an artist."

"More important than money? What could be..." Wait. The new Kathleen knew the answer. Fulfillment was more important. Love was far more important. She'd spent seventy-five thousand dollars for a chance—not even a guarantee—at that happiness.

And the minutes were slipping away.

She dragged herself back to immediate concerns. "I'll see you later. I've got to go to Hannah. Alone."

Firmly, he repeated, "I'm coming with you. I was part of the problem, and I won't desert you now."

"Why?"

"Because it's the right thing to do."

"You don't know what you're getting into. She's—"

"What? A fire-breathing dragon?" he scoffed. "Hey, princess, I wouldn't be much of a knight in shining armor if I turned tail and ran at the first sign of battle."

"Battle, huh?" A fairly accurate description, she thought. "Listen, Foster, you may be joking, but you don't know my mother. Maybe she won't blowtorch your face, but the woman has perfected the art of tongue-lashing. You'll be flayed within an inch of your self-respect. And you don't have to do it. Why would you? I don't get it."

"It's called integrity." The slight smile that curved the corners of his lips was wry and self-deprecating. "Let's face it. I'm not the kind of guy who's ever going to have a statue erected to commemorate his character. But my grandma taught me not to lie, not to cheat and not to desert my friends when they need help." He took out the pocket watch again. "It's seven-fifty. Let's get this over with before the rest of the office staff arrives."

Giving up, she followed him into the building, somewhat worried. Foster's burst of loyalty was troublesome. Her plan for the day had been to seduce him, to convince him that she was the woman for him. She most certainly did not want to drag him into a squabble with Hannah. After all, if things worked out between them and they formed a real relationship, there would be plenty of time for family disputes later.

At the door to her mother's office, she paused to get her bearings. For the past year, this had been her own office. Her mother's secretary, Helen, had been her secretary. It would be strange to be standing on the other side of the president's desk. She tapped lightly, then entered, with Foster right behind her. "Mom, I'm sorry about what just happened."

"I demand an explanation for your open defiance, Kathleen. Without any of your usual excuses."

Hannah's dark brown eyes glittered like obsidian. Beneath her shoulder pads, she seemed formidable and strong. Wonderfully strong, Kathleen thought. A feeling of pure joy rose up inside her, bringing a smile to her lips. It was good to see her mother this way. For a year, Kathleen had watched her mother suffer while she retrained her devastated body, slowly forcing herself from the bed, learning to walk again while holding Kathleen's arm. Hannah's good health—now, at this moment—was cause to rejoice.

"Young lady," her mother snapped, "why are you grinning?"

"Sorry, Mother." This very afternoon at four-fifteen, Hannah would be stricken—unless Kathleen could prevent it. She tried to keep her tone nonconfrontational, to maintain a low stress level. "I'll try to explain. Foster and I had to come to the store late last night. We were both exhausted, so we went upstairs."

"Why did you need to come to the store?"

"That's my fault," Zach said, stepping forward. "Kathleen got her hair cut, and I'm not quite done with her portrait. We were looking for a wig."

"Ah, yes. The portrait." Hannah's face was without expression, but her voice seemed to sneer. "Artwork by a window dresser. Why should I be expected to take this nonsense seriously?"

"Because," Kathleen defended, "Foster *is* an artist."

"Come now, dear. If Mr. Foster was a true artist, why isn't he pursuing contacts in New York, or Paris, or even Santa Fe? Why is he working here in Denver?"

"Mother—" Kathleen began, but Foster touched her arm, restraining her.

"A valid question," he said. "I work here for reasons I think you could understand, Mrs. Welles."

"Oh?" Her penciled eyebrows lifted in two perfect arches. Her fingers toyed with the strand of pearls around her throat. "Do you presume that you and I have common interests?"

"I presume that we're both pretty damned stubborn. You're keeping your department store open in a city where people shop in malls. Downtown Denver is not Fifth Avenue in New York. It's not even State Street in Chicago. Why not close down, Mrs. Welles?"

"The malls are a fad," she said. "This store has years of tradition."

"But not much profit," he pressed. "You stubbornly stay open because of sentiment and your own beliefs. I respect that, ma'am. I've done the same."

Her cheeks flushed crimson. "How dare you—a no one, a nothing—compare yourself to me and to Welles, Incorporated? You're fired, Mr. Foster."

"Not necessary. I quit, Mrs. Welles." He took two steps toward the door, then pivoted back toward her. "But don't go too hard on Kathleen. She's a good daughter."

With a gracious bow toward Hannah and a wink at Kathleen, he left.

"Good riddance," Hannah muttered.

Kathleen stared at the closed door. He'd left. He'd quit. How on earth would this turn of events affect the year to come...which was really the year that had already happened?

She desperately wanted to run after him. But she couldn't leave her mother. Not until she convinced

Hannah to make an appointment with Dr. Mathers, a task that would take all her new negotiating skills.

"Kathleen, I forbid you to see that...that reprobate again."

"Mother, please." Still distracted, she gazed longingly at the exit. "This is the twentieth century, and I'm twenty-six years old."

"Twenty-five," Hannah corrected. "Just think, dear, you're a quarter of a century old. It's time you start seriously considering marriage."

Kathleen's head whipped around on her neck. Hannah's words commanded her attention. This was exactly how their argument had started one year ago! With talk of marriage. *A quarter of a century...it's time...marriage.*

This time, Kathleen must not allow herself to be provoked to fight back. No matter what her mother said, she would remain sane and reasonable. Her mother's health was at stake.

Hannah continued. "You need to look at men in a different way now. To stop this childish rebellion. For once in your life, use your judgment."

"I do, Mother. I make it a point to avoid men who bore me." Kathleen frowned and gnawed at her lower lip. Those were the words she'd said before. Was she powerless to control herself? Would she be forced to make the same mistakes twice?

"There are worse things than boredom."

"Yes, there are." Kathleen called upon her experience of the past year. There was regret. There was pain. There was heartache. She curbed her arguments. "I understand, Mother. And perhaps you're right. I'll definitely give it some more thought," she placated.

"Ask yourself these questions," Hannah advised. "Will he embarrass me at social occasions? Will he be a help or a hindrance to Welles? Will the man I choose be a good father for my children? A good, reliable provider for them? It *is* time to be thinking of children, Kathleen."

"Heirs," she said. "I know."

"What do you know?"

"Unless I have children, our ownership shares in Welles will eventually be inherited by distant cousins."

"Exactly." Hannah said. "And we both know that your cousins would delight in selling the store to the highest bidder."

A year ago, Kathleen might not have cared one iota about the distant future of the store.

A year ago, she'd felt little interest in the perpetuation of the Welles dynasty.

But now?

After acting as president for twelve months, she'd seen how tight the profit margins were. And she'd become competitive. Some of her advertising programs had been absolute coups. Other strategies were mistakes that made the opening of the ill-fated Denver International Airport look like a smooth business move. But she was trying, fighting for the survival of the family business.

"I won't let the store close down," she said. "Believe me, Mother. I love Welles."

Hannah's dark eyes widened, and she folded her arms beneath her breasts. "I've never heard you say anything like that before. I'm very pleased, Kathleen."

Pushing her momentary advantage, like a general who'd massed her troops for an ambush, Kathleen commanded the topic of conversation. "I'm glad I've made you happy, Mother. Because, frankly, I'm a little worried about you. You don't look well. Are you feeling all right? Isn't it about time for your annual physical?"

"Not for another month."

"That's why you came to work so early, isn't it? You couldn't sleep. You were uncomfortable."

"It's the heat," she said. "The summer always makes me a bit uncomfortable. And this season, well, it's difficult."

Kathleen should have guessed. They were rapidly approaching the Fourth of July weekend, the date, ten years ago, when her father and brother had been killed in the car accident. If Hannah herself could have gone back in time, she certainly would have selected that day. She would have kept her husband and son off the road. She would have kept them safe.

"I'll be all right," Hannah said. "I came in early because I have quite a bit of work to accomplish today. I'd left some of it upstairs."

"Where you and my father used to go," Kathleen mused. Her mother and father had been happy in their private nest above the store. Perhaps Hannah went there when she especially missed him. Perhaps she had some unconscious hint of her own impending stroke and was looking to the past for strength.

"Tell you what, Mother. I'll arrange with Helen for you to have a checkup today, anyway."

"Don't be absurd. I'm fine."

"Please, Mother. You've got to take care of yourself. Please."

"Out of the question. I've got too much to do." To emphasize her words, Hannah picked up a stack of papers and centered them on the desk in front of her. "This conversation is over, Kathleen. And I expect you to sever this infatuation with Mr. Foster and look for a suitable mate."

Kathleen pretended to acquiesce, stepped toward the door and rested her hand on the doorknob. Clearly, she needed to call upon all her newly acquired negotiating skills to convince her mother to visit the doctor. This situation should be easy, because Kathleen was well aware of Hannah's Achilles' heel.

Still at the door, she murmured, "If you don't care about your appearance…"

"What did you say?"

"Oh, nothing. Don't mind me." Kathleen was the picture of innocence.

"You said something about my appearance."

"Well, Mother, I hate to say this, but..."

"What is it?" Hannah fished in her top desk drawer, took out a compact and flipped it open to study her reflection in the small mirror. "Is there something wrong with the way I look?"

"You're haggard, Mother. You don't look well. You see? Even concealer can't cover the circles under your eyes. Your eyes are dull. Those little tiny lines around your mouth are deeper, almost etched."

Hannah lightly pressed her skin. "Do I look puffy?"

"Exactly," Kathleen said. "But what can you expect? We both know that good health is the first step toward beauty, and when you're ignoring your physical symptoms..."

"I look haggard?" Her vanity was pricked. "Do I?"

"I don't mean to be nasty. After all, you're beautifully slim. But there's a paleness, a pasty quality to your skin, and a lack of sheen in your hair." It was a safe bet to assume her mother was on a diet. Hannah was always dieting. "Have you been eating properly?"

"Perhaps not."

"I really think you should see a doctor. Today."

Though Hannah eyed her daughter suspiciously, she submitted to Kathleen's suggestion. "Oh, all right. If Dr. Armitage can fit me in."

Here was another problem. Dr. Armitage had been the family doctor for years and years. Though he was fine as a general practitioner, her mother needed a specialist. The doctor who would treat her after the stroke was Gregory Mathers. "I've heard of another doctor who's very good. Several of my friends have started going to him."

"Dr. Armitage is fine with me."

"Do let me check with this other doctor. He's a specialist, and I—"

"Don't push it, Kathleen." Her tone indicated a dismissal. "I've said I will visit Dr. Armitage, and that is final."

"I'll arrange it with Helen."

When Kathleen stepped into the outer office area, the time was precisely eight-thirty, and she didn't even have to check her wristwatch to know the hour. During the past year, while she'd been acting president, Kathleen had learned the established routine. The rest of the office staff reported for work at nine, but it was exactly half past eight when Helen placed her full coffee mug on a coaster and flicked her computer on, a full thirty minutes before the Welles department store was open for business.

"Good morning, Helen."

"Kathleen."

Though her mother's secretary must have been shocked to the roots of her silver gray hair, Helen was much too disciplined to register visible astonishment at seeing Kathleen, the errant Welles daughter, in the offices so early. "Helen, I need your help."

"Yes?" She swiveled in her secretary's chair, her pen poised above the yellow legal pad where she kept endless lists. "What is it, Kathleen?"

"My mother needs a doctor's appointment, for today. The earlier, the better. Try for one o'clock."

"I'll see that Dr. Armitage fits her in."

No doubt, she would. Helen was capable of rearranging the schedule of an entire hospital if the end result benefited Welles. "But I'd rather that Hannah see a different doctor. His name is Gregory Mathers." Kathleen recited his phone number from memory. After her mother's stroke, she'd talked with Mathers at least once a week.

"It's not my place to criticize," Helen said, "but your mother has gone to Dr. Armitage for years."

"I know. And he's a fine physician."

"Then why the change?"

For a moment, Kathleen paused. She knew that half-truths did not work well with this highly practical woman. Telling the whole truth was, of course, impossible. Time travel? Helen would as likely believe Kathleen had been captured by aliens and beamed to Alpha Centuri.

There was not, however, much recourse. Taking a deep breath, Kathleen said, "Unless you and I can stop the course of fate, my mother will suffer a devastating stroke this afternoon at four-fifteen. Dr. Mathers is a specialist. I hope, with his expertise, he will recognize the symptoms and treat my mother."

Helen digested the information and, apparently, found it to be sound. She nodded once. "Dr. Mathers, it is."

That was simple. Perhaps too simple. "Helen, do you know something I don't?"

"Many things, I'm sure. For example, the year-to-date financial statement for Welles."

Kathleen remembered the hot-pink brochure that had mysteriously appeared on her desk. Without postmark or envelope. "Do you know a woman named Diana Marie Casey?"

"Doesn't ring a bell."

"Perhaps a chime? Like the chime from—"

"A clock tower?" Helen finished the sentence. "No, I can't say that it does."

She knew something. Kathleen was certain and, somehow, reassured. She sensed that in Helen she had a cohort, albeit a secret one, on her quest to put things right. "Thank you, Helen."

"I want what's best for you, Kathleen, and for your mother. And for the store, of course."

Her slight frown indicated that the conversation was over. Helen made a check beside an item on her legal pad and reached for the telephone console on her desk.

"I'll try to talk with Dr. Mathers after you've arranged the appointment," Kathleen said. "Please call me on my cellular phone when—"

"I have the time set."

"And would you notify my office that I won't—"

"Be in for the rest of the day," Helen said. Then she smiled broadly. "Everything will be all right, Kathleen. Don't you worry."

For the first time since she'd journeyed back in time, Kathleen began to believe it. Everything *would* be okay.

On the drive back to her condo, Kathleen considered her agenda for the rest of the day. Every second of her time needed to be spent judiciously.

Since she planned to seduce Foster into loving her eternally, she needed, first off, to get him alone again, away from his motley crew of assistants and the gallery people who would surely be demanding his attention today. This might be a difficult task. And yet, Hannah had inadvertently helped Kathleen's cause by firing him. At least, Foster wouldn't have a Welles crisis to handle.

The seduction itself was more complicated. Kathleen needed to set the stage for romance. She wanted something that would excite his senses *and* engage his emotions. There had to be music. Fine food. Mentally, she made a note to contact Jean-Pierre, who was a fabulous caterer. And the surroundings, the ambiance, needed to be special, artistic, unforgettable.

Not a restaurant. Not a dinner at home in her condo. Not even a picnic in the mountains.

While she changed clothes, selecting a sundress that lightly skimmed her body, she made phone calls. Jean-Pierre was first on the list. Then, a limousine service. Finally, she called a woman she'd worked with on several charity functions.

Her strategy was complex. Nothing could be left to chance. She must succeed. She had less than a day to secure eternity.

The earliest time for all her arrangements to be put into effect was five o'clock. That was good, Kathleen thought, because by then she would no longer have to worry about her mother. The time of Hannah's stroke would have passed.

But those last hours, from five until midnight, would be highly pressured. Was it enough time?

It had to be. She would make every minute count.

Chapter Five

Using her cellular phone, Kathleen telephoned Foster's window-design office, a storefront three blocks away from his studio, while she was on her way there. One of his assistants—the people Helen referred to as thugs—answered.

"Windows of My Mind," the voice said. The name of Foster's business seemed to change depending upon who picked up the phone.

"I'd like to speak with Foster, please. This is Kathleen."

"Ms. Welles, huh? This is Donny—remember me?"

"Yes, I do." According to Helen, Donny was one of the worst dress-code offenders, with three earrings in one ear and several tattoos. "How are you, Donny?"

"I'm cool. Hey, I bet you're calling to say you're sorry about firing us."

"You're not fired. Not really. It was just a tiff."

"A what?"

"A spat." The silence on the other end of the phone told her that she still wasn't communicating with this tattooed airhead. Why on earth did Foster hire these misfits? "A meaningless argument."

"Got it. Cool."

"May I talk with Foster?"

"He's not here. He's, like, over at Kendall Gallery."

"Thanks."

Kathleen negotiated several lane changes through the rush-hour traffic and headed farther downtown. This area had changed radically since the brand-new baseball stadium had been built. Derelict buildings had been torn down or renovated into upscale lofts, pubs and galleries offering crafts, jewelry and fine artwork. Kendall Gallery was among the largest and the most well-respected.

She offered thanks to the parking gods for allowing her to find a space right in front. Through the large plate-glass window, she saw Foster talking to a tall, gaunt, bearded man with a stooping posture that brought to mind a praying mantis.

But she proceeded to ignore that man. With Foster in sight, no one else existed. Kathleen exhaled a heavy sigh more typical of a teenager with a crush than an adult woman with a twenty-four-hour mission. He wore his usual Levi's and a white oxford-cloth shirt that emphasized his tanned ruggedness. His long sleeves were pushed up to the elbows, revealing sinewed forearms. As he gestured, she saw the strength in his hands, and she remembered the fiery passion in his touch when he'd caressed her that morning. He reached up to loosen his necktie, a splash of ocean blue. If she'd had to choose a fashion description for him, it would be casual elegance. Not fashionable. Certainly not trendy. Because Foster was an original, more special than the fabulous clothing in the Welles designer salon.

As she entered the gallery, his voice reverberated in the cavernous display area and sank deep into her soul. The words were unimportant. It was the deep, rich baritone that struck chords within her. How she longed to hear that voice whispering endearments and promises of a future together.

"I can't do it without permission," he said to the bearded mantis. "It's not my problem that one of your other artists didn't deliver on time."

"But this is an opportunity for you, Foster. I'm telling you that I have space for three more paintings."

"And I'm telling you that I'm not sure if I can fill the space."

"Don't turn me down," the gallery owner warned. "This showing is going to be a big hit. Tomorrow night, you're going to meet influential people, people with money."

Foster said nothing, and the bearded man continued. "For the past month you've been bragging about your current project, how it's the best work you've ever done. And now you turn me down?"

"I'll see what I can do."

"Are you crazy? Well, sure you are. All artists are crazy. But you've got business sense. I know you do. So listen to me. I'm giving you the chance to show these paintings, your best work ever."

"There's someone else who needs to approve."

"What?" He staggered and clutched his chest as if he'd been shot in the heart. "Don't tell me you got an agent."

"Look, it's too complicated to explain. I'll let you know about the paintings."

Kathleen knew exactly what they were talking about, and a fearsome ambivalence shook her. The topic of Foster's three paintings was something she had hoped to avoid until after she'd ensured he was in love with her. She was tempted to sneak out the door before he saw her, but she didn't want to stay away from him. These moments were special, and she wanted to be with him. She cleared her throat, frantically thinking of an excuse that could deter his inevitable request of her.

He turned and saw her, and his lips curved in a lazy, sexy grin. His blue eyes warmed, raising her body temperature several degrees. "Kathleen." Her name sounded romantic when he spoke it. "How's your mother?"

"I think she'll be all right." Reining her desires, she pulled the cellular phone from her purse. "I'm waiting for a message."

He introduced her to the gallery owner, who fawned politely when he heard the name Welles. "Will you be coming to our show tomorrow night?"

"I don't know," she said with absolute honesty. "I'll try."

Foster ushered her to the door. "I'll get back to you on those paintings," he promised the owner.

They stood on the street outside the gallery with the heat of summer surrounding them. Activity came slowly to this part of town, where there were few office buildings. After nightfall, the area came alive. But at nine-thirty in the morning, there weren't many retail customers on the streets.

"Beautiful day," Foster said, glancing up into the cloudless heavens, a sky nearly as blue as his eyes.

"I've planned a dinner for us," she said. "Tonight at five o'clock. I hope that's okay with you."

"It's fine. But—"

"And I thought, until then, we could—"

"I'm going to be fairly busy today, Kathleen."

"Why?" she questioned. "If I'm not mistaken, your business with the gallery owner sounded pretty much concluded."

"Pretty much," he agreed. "There are only three more paintings I need to deliver."

She continued quickly, not allowing him to say more about those paintings. "And doing the windows at Welles for our weekend sale is no longer on your agenda."

"Yeah. That's too bad. I like to keep my assistants busy."

"Well, you won't be fired forever. In fact, I'm sure your services will be reinstated before the day is over. Give your workers—and yourself—the day off. You and I can spend it together."

He regarded her through hooded eyes. "That's a little autocratic of you, don't you think?"

"What's the use of being a princess if I don't make any demands?"

He laughed. "You got me there. First, I'll have to head over to the office and tell the guys what's up. I'll meet you there. My van's parked a couple of blocks away."

A quick glance up and down the street showed ample parking. It seemed strange that he had been unable to find a spot nearby. "I'll walk with you," she said.

He set out with long strides, and she hurried to keep up. Around the corner they went, then left, then down two blocks. Suddenly, a sense of foreboding reached out with icy fingers to clutch at Kathleen. In the midst of the summer heat, she shivered. Even before they arrived, she knew their destination. Her gaze lifted, and she saw the stone gargoyles on the building where she'd met Diana Marie Casey. Foster's van was parked in front.

"I had a delivery here." He pointed to the sign hanging above the entryway. "That's it."

A thick rim of filigreed metal encircled a white clock face with black Roman numerals. A coincidence? She looked closely at him, searched his face for clues. But he appeared to be utterly nonchalant.

She cleared her throat, matching his ease, and said, "The sign resembles your grandmother's pocket watch, enlarged about a hundred times. What kind of shop is this?"

"The lady's a clock maker," Foster explained. "For some reason, she didn't want her name on the sign."

"The lady?" She fought back the chill of apprehension, fought the fear. "Diana Marie Casey?"

"I don't know her first name. Her last name is van Winkle. Cute, huh? Like Rip van Winkle, who slept for a hundred years. And the shop is called Time Merchants."

Even though he'd said the words, Foster seemed to make no connection to *her* time merchant. He had gone around to the driver's side of the van, but Kathleen stood rooted to the sidewalk, unable to move, afraid to stay.

"Kathleen? Is something wrong?" he asked.

For some reason, she'd been drawn back here, summoned from her day in the past to meet once again with the woman who'd sold it to her. She could not think of any positive, uplifting reason Diana Marie would want to see her again. This had to be bad news. Still, she could not ignore the invitation. Compelled, as if in a trance, she walked toward the entryway. Her feet, in light sandals, felt heavy as bricks.

"Kathleen? What is it?"

"Time," she said. "I need to buy some time."

"You mean a clock? Well, this van Winkle woman has a great selection."

Foster came up beside her, taking his place at her side as if he belonged there. His presence comforted her, and she wished she could confide in him. She wanted so much to share with him, to draw upon his strength. But it was too soon.

Kathleen opened the door and stepped into the foyer with grandfather clocks on each side. It was the same as it had been—or would be, one year in the future.

Without pause, she ascended the long staircase and pushed open the door. Though the room was filled with an assortment of clocks and timepieces, the arrangement was different, more suitable for a shop, with a long glass counter displaying wristwatches. She saw no one.

Tension, cold and stark, raised goose bumps on her bare arms. There was nothing here but . . . time.

The clocks ticked, not quite in unison. The gravity of Kathleen's undertaking weighed heavy as a blanket of wet snow. How had she ever thought she could change the past? Life wasn't meant to be thus. Was she making mistakes, causing even more turmoil by tampering with events that had already occurred? She sensed that her presence here in the past was dangerous.

Foster touched her waist, and she started, jumpy as a colt.

"What's wrong?" he asked.

She could tell him. Could reveal everything. But her secret knowledge seemed to isolate her at the very moment when she desperately needed a companion. Again, she was tempted. *Tell him. Tell him everything.*

Peering into his attentive blue eyes, she remembered the way it would be in the future, the anger she would see in the depths of those eyes. A shudder convulsed her shoulders. She couldn't bear his hatred. Not again.

If she failed in this day, if he did not learn to love her within this twenty-four-hour period, she would be devastated. She needed to use caution in building their relationship. She needed his trust.

A familiar voice interrupted her thoughts. "Have you found what you're looking for?"

Kathleen stared. The name Diana Marie was on the tip of her tongue, but the woman who stood before her was not that flamboyant female. The bespectacled Mrs. van Winkle was white-haired, dressed in a conservative navy blue suit.

"An hourglass," Kathleen said. "With an ornate rosewood frame and sands that sparkle like gold dust."

"I could make such a timepiece," she said.

"Are you sure you don't have one? Perhaps in the back room?"

"Afraid not, miss."

When the woman removed her gold-framed glasses, Kathleen recognized the dark black eyes of Diana Marie. She'd changed form, hidden her magic in the guise of a mild, elderly shopkeeper, but Mrs. van Winkle was the same woman. But how could that be? Kathleen wondered if she were dreaming, if Mrs. van Winkle was an illusion. What was happening? Why? Anger sparked within her. She'd bought this day and paid a high price. Diana Marie had no right to intrude.

Mrs. van Winkle turned toward Foster. "Hello again, Mr. Foster. It's so nice to see you. Is this your wife?"

"My friend," Foster said. As if nothing were amiss, he introduced the two of them. "Kathleen Welles, meet Mrs. van Winkle."

The woman held out a soft white hand scented with lavender. "Miss Welles? How else may I be of service?"

"You tell me." Kathleen gripped her hand. The flesh was solid, not a fantasy. Her sense of touch told her the woman existed in physical reality. In an abrupt, almost rude tone, Kathleen demanded an answer. "Why am I here?"

"How would I know? I'm not a fortune-teller." The lively black eyes danced in an old woman's face, teasing and laughing. But the voice, though trembly with age, seemed to hold a threat. "Frankly, if you don't care for my wares, it might be better if you went back where you came from."

"Not yet. I'm not ready."

"Perhaps I should mention that when you purchase any of my merchandise, if you are dissatisfied, I am willing to offer a refund. A partial refund."

"But you don't offer any guarantees, do you?"

"Oh, no. I don't believe in meaningless promises. Everything breaks down. Even the most perfect timepiece."

"Is that what's happening? Is there a breakdown?"

By now Kathleen's head was spinning. Logic was topsy-turvy. Their conversation carried layer upon layer of meaning. And Kathleen was certain that she was missing something, some esoteric message. Was Diana Marie telling her she had to go back to the future? Had something in her time-merchanting business gone awry?

Foster touched her hand, linked his fingers with hers. Immediately, she felt grounded, stronger. He cared for her. Of that, she was certain. But could he ever return her eternal love?

"I think we ought to go," he said. To Mrs. van Winkle, he added, "Sorry to trouble you."

"No trouble at all. This is my life's work."

"Come on, Kathleen." He tugged at her hand.

She felt disoriented, paralyzed. Yet she was in motion, as if she were free-falling through time and space. Something whistled at the edges of her mind, like an ill wind.

Was there a future beyond this moment? Was any of this real? She had so desperately wanted the past to change that she might have imagined this complex scenario of time merchants and reliving a day. Was she crazy? Had her grief driven her mad?

Her heart beat fast. A cold sweat broke on her forehead. These sensations were not intangible. She was here. Now. Kathleen reached with her free hand and touched the glass display case. It felt smooth and solid, had form and shape. If she struck the surface, it would shatter.

As if from far away, she heard Foster's voice asking if she was all right, if she wanted to sit down. Did he care? Did he really care about her? His voice held concern, but was his kindness anything more than a gesture? Damn, nothing was clear. Nothing made sense.

Her clever negotiation with Diana Marie had trapped her. Was this all a hoax? A conspiracy? Was everyone—Helen, Mrs. van Winkle, Foster himself— all in on the joke? Having a good laugh at her expense? But why, why, why?

She gripped his hand so tightly that her fingers went numb. She would not lose him. If she were drawn back into a time warp, she would take him with her.

Her vision blurred, and she shook her head to clear the dark fear that seemed to close around her. Gulping down deep breaths, Kathleen drew on every bit of willpower and determination she had honed over the past year of handling the department store. She was strong enough to face this damned nightmare.

The clocks chimed, and she focused her gaze on Mrs. van Winkle. Fighting the panic, Kathleen said, "I have many more hours."

The elderly woman replaced her glasses on the bridge of her nose. "To be sure. And perhaps a lifetime to regret them."

"What do you mean?"

"Imagine yourself running a race. You don't come in last, but you're somewhere in the middle of the pack. Such a race is easy to forget." She smiled sweetly. "Isn't that so, Mr. Foster?"

He said nothing. Kathleen glanced up at him and saw the hard edge of anger that she'd come to know so well. This time, however, his hostility was directed toward Diana Marie.

She continued. "Now imagine another race, Miss Welles. Imagine yourself putting forth your best effort, straining with all your might. And you come in second. You lose by one pace, one inch, one instant. That loss is far greater pain. Wouldn't you think so, Mr. Foster?"

Something very weird was happening here. Zach didn't know what it was, but his instincts told him to take care of Kathleen. She needed him. She was pale. Her eyelids blinked rapidly, as if she were fighting off unconsciousness. He braced his arm around her slender waist, holding her so she wouldn't faint. Her body was tense, every muscle strung tight.

"Let's get out of here, Kathleen."

Her beautiful eyes were wide and frightened. Her voice trembled. "I have to win the race, Foster. I have to come in first."

"You will," he assured her. Her mood was too intense to be taken lightly. "Whatever it is that you need to do, Kathleen, you can do it."

"Oh, Miss Welles," Mrs. van Winkle said, "you'd better answer that."

"Answer what?" Zach hadn't heard anything. Then Kathleen's cellular phone buzzed from the depths of her purse. Why hadn't he heard it on the first ring? Had the phone even made a sound?

While Kathleen shakily dealt with her phone call, he scrutinized Mrs. van Winkle. She'd shown up at his office last week and described the sign she wanted, insisting that it be delivered today, early in the morning.

Though he'd questioned why she'd chosen him—he was not a professional sign painter—and questioned the wisdom of using a sign instead of an actual working clock, she'd said she wanted an artistic representation, and she paid in cash. So he'd painted the clock face, using his grandmother's pocket watch for a model. And he'd drawn the hands at five o'clock—everybody's favorite time, quitting time.

Kathleen's voice was stronger when she spoke again. "A change in plans, Foster. We need to go to the golf course."

"For a match?"

"For a doctor." Turning to Mrs. van Winkle, she said simply, "Goodbye."

"I'll see you again, Miss Welles. Maybe sooner than you think."

Those parting words sounded like a threat, Zach thought. But why? What had Kathleen's encounter with this elderly lady meant? When he glanced at Mrs. van Winkle, he saw another view, like a shadow. Behind her, he glimpsed the distinctive shape of an hourglass. Holding the glass, head thrown back, laughing wildly, was a woman dressed in a long skirt and flowing scarves.

He looked more closely, and the vision vanished, leaving only a small gray-haired woman. Mrs. van Winkle. "Goodbye, Mr. Foster."

He hurried along with Kathleen and held her arm as they descended the steep staircase. "What's going on?"

"That was Helen, my mother's secretary, on the phone," she explained. "I told her to make an appointment with Dr. Gregory Mathers for my mother. But Mathers is playing golf until two o'clock this afternoon. That's cutting it too close."

"Too close for what?"

"I want my mother to see him by one." She pushed open the door to the street. Her complexion was still bloodless and white, but her jaw was set and her eyes were clear. "The timing is important. Can we take your van?"

"Sure, but—"

He halted, staring up at the sign in disbelief. He had drawn the hands at five o'clock. But the painted hands showed the time to be twenty-two minutes past ten. "What the hell?"

Kathleen stood at the passenger side of his van. "Hurry, Foster. We don't have much time."

He took his grandmother's watch from his pocket. The hands exactly matched the time shown on the sign. But his grandmother's watch hands kept moving. One minute at a time. On the clock, time stood still.

"Foster, please hurry."

When he looked up at the clock sign, the painted hands had moved again. When he'd looked away, the hands had crept to another position. Something very strange, very wrong, was happening here. Zach didn't believe in magic, but that's what this appeared to be. Dark magic.

He went around the van and slid into the driver's seat. When he looked at the sign again, the hands were back at five o'clock, exactly the way he'd painted them. He shook his head. "Kathleen, take a look at that sign. Where are the hands?"

"On five o'clock. Why?"

"I thought I saw something very weird. But I guess not." He keyed the ignition and started up the van. "Where are we going?"

"To the Platte Country Club, on the south end of town." Apparently, Kathleen had recovered. Her attitude was now one filled with purpose. "If we have to hog-tie this doctor and strap a stethoscope to his ears, that's what we'll do. He will see my mother before one o'clock today."

"What's so important about the timing?"

"I can't tell you. I just know."

He eased the van into the street and headed south. "This has something to do with your fortune-teller's magic. When I was in Mrs. van Winkle's shop, I even thought *I* saw her."

"Diana Marie?"

"A dark woman dressed in flowing scarves, holding an hourglass."

"Oh, my God," Kathleen gasped.

Her eyes held a bittersweet sheen, a combination of hopefulness and apprehension. Caught between joy and sorrow, laughter and tears, she was mysterious and beautiful. And she inspired him. He wanted to paint her. Now. At this moment.

"You saw her," she said. "Oh, Foster, that's such a relief. I'd almost convinced myself that I'd gone crazy. Did you really see her?"

"I don't know." He cleared his throat. "To tell you the truth, Kathleen, I wouldn't make too much of this. Maybe I'm so tired, I was hallucinating."

"Describe the hourglass."

His memory for visual detail was, of course, excellent. "The wood frame was dark red. Mahogany or rosewood. Ornate carving, maybe cherubs. And the sands flashed and shimmered, almost half through."

He paused. "Isn't that like the hourglass you asked Mrs. van Winkle for?"

"You saw it?" she questioned.

"I don't know. It was an impression." He snapped back to the reality of traffic and city noise. "What the hell is going on?"

Chapter Six

"An hourglass," she repeated. Was Foster's vision a warning?

She should have been reassured by the idea that she was not alone in this web of weird magic, that Foster had also been ensnared. Instead, she was nervous.

"Okay, Kathleen, I want some answers."

She glanced at her wristwatch. He sounded impatient, and she was anxious. If she launched into the whole story, debated with him, as she would no doubt have to, they would waste precious time. "It's all too unbelievable."

"I'll decide what to believe and what not to believe. What was all that business about a race?"

"It was about time, okay? Like a race where every millisecond counts. Time." She felt herself sinking into fear again, and she fought the feeling. "Foster, if you could live one day of your life over again, would you?"

"Yes," he said quickly. Then he reconsidered. "No, I guess I wouldn't. Because one day could change everything else, and I wouldn't want to take the chance on living a different future. My life is okay. Not perfect, but okay."

"But what if this one day, one twenty-four-hour period, was perfectly horrible? The worst day of your life?"

He shook his head. "There are usually pluses to match every minus."

"A silver lining to every cloud," she suggested.

"Right."

Try as she might, Kathleen could not think of one single positive aspect that had resulted from that June twenty-first when she'd first lived it. Except... possibly...that the day had forced her to grow up and deal with her responsibilities as an adult. She was different now. No question about that. If she changed everything, would she revert to being a childish, spoiled princess? In losing the depth of her despair, would she also lose her hard-won maturity?

She shuddered to think of going back to that flighty, boring existence. Being a spoiled, pampered princess was nowhere near as satisfying as exercising her brain and her will, setting goals and accomplishing them. She'd never thought of that. The growth that came from her pain. Still, to let her mother suffer if she could somehow prevent it...

"Kathleen?"

"Tonight, I'll explain everything," she said. "After dinner." By then, she would know if he was intended to be her eternal love or not. By then, she'd have the answers she'd risked so much to find. "Trust me."

"I hate when people say that." His eyebrows drew into a stern line. His strong, capable hands tightly gripped the steering wheel.

She longed to unburden herself, to lean on him, to accept the protection he'd offered when they were in the presence of Mrs. van Winkle. But that wasn't her purpose for the day. She'd undertaken this journey alone, to right her own wrongs, and she well remembered what it was like to have Foster despise her. She could only tell him the truth when she was sure he loved her. After her goal had been achieved.

Noticing the streets around her, Kathleen realized they weren't going to the golf course. When she started giving directions, he interrupted. "I have to stop by the office first. I'll be a lot better off if I have the machine answer the phone instead of Donny."

"Agreed. Every time I call, he's got a different answer. Windows of My Mind. Window Vipers. Windows Bar and Grill. Really, Foster, it's terribly unprofessional. Why don't you talk to him about it?"

"I'd rather let the kid have his fun. Donny is my number-one assistant."

"Why is that?"

"He's basically a good kid, supporting his mother and a younger brother who's doing well in high school and might actually make something of himself." He shrugged. "And mostly because Donny has a car that usually makes it to appointments on time."

"You will hurry, won't you? We need to get to that golf course and find Dr. Mathers."

"I'll be quick. My office is on the way."

"Okay." She settled back in the passenger seat. It probably would have been smarter to fetch her own car and drive herself. But then, she might have been away from Foster for hours. And they needed this time together.

So much had to be packed into these twenty-four hours. In addition to her elaborate plans for seduction, she wanted to learn every detail she could about Zachary Foster, the man she already loved. Now was her chance. Perhaps her only chance...

"You have a very odd group of young men working for you," she said, simulating a sane conversational tone despite all the turmoil within her. "Helen thinks they're hooligans."

"Helen's right."

"Oh, come on." She forced a chuckle. "You're much too good a businessman to hire a crew of thugs."

"But I have. These guys—and two girls, though you couldn't guess their gender by looking at them—are not your stereotypical all-American youth. They're dropouts, juvenile offenders, troublemakers. But after they've been with me for a couple of months, they pick up some skills."

It was a relief to engage in rational business talk. She pondered the logic behind Foster's employment scheme. "Sounds like a lot of work for you. Why do you do it?"

"Why not?"

He turned off Colfax Avenue, past a seedy liquor store on the corner, and within blocks they were in the midst of mansions. "I like to give these kids a chance," he said. "Don't get me wrong. I don't consider myself a one-man rehabilitation center. If they goof off, they're out. But as long as they are willing to try, I'm willing to employ them."

She suspected there was something more personal. "Could it be that, at one time, you were a little thug yourself?"

"Never." He grinned. "I was always big for my age. A large thug."

"Tell me more."

"It's not real exciting. I had the classic lower-class upbringing. My father took off before I was born. Mama died when I was nine. Three years later, I got picked up for shoplifting and stealing a car. I got expelled from junior high for fighting."

"All this when you were twelve?"

"Yeah."

Such a life seemed alien to Kathleen, who had been sheltered in boarding schools. Her concept of crime was cheating on a biology test or borrowing her mother's clothes without permission. And yet, she knew the devastating trauma of losing even one parent. Such an event could cast a child hopelessly adrift. When her father passed away, she was lucky enough to be in safe waters. "Your grandmother took care of you then?"

"Yeah," he said. "I had two younger brothers, and we were all pretty wild, but Grandma taught us right from wrong. Not that her lessons sank in right away. I'm sorry to say that we put that good woman through hell. If it hadn't been for Father Blaize over at the church, she probably would have given up."

"Father Blaize? The name is familiar."

"He's involved in most of the charity work in town. For a priest, he's fairly political."

"Is he the one who set you on the path toward being an artist?"

"Eventually. But for a while there, I wouldn't listen to anybody. I was only into graffiti."

"Graffiti?"

"For a couple of years, I was king of the spray can. No Dumpster in town was safe. Then Father Blaize introduced me to oil painting and gave me a push."

He parked in front of his storefront, where a dancing mannequin held sway amid an artfully wild display of flowers.

He escorted Kathleen inside. Two large desks and a bank of metal file cabinets might have made the place an average-looking office, except that the walls were covered with sketches and photographs. Kathleen noticed a young man wearing a headband and a sleeveless T-shirt that displayed a tattoo of a bleeding broken heart. The boy aimed an automatic pistol at Kathleen, saying cheerily, "Welcome to Wasted Windows."

Foster stepped around her and snatched the weapon. "Not funny, Donny."

"Gimme a break, man. It's only a toy. It's plastic. Got it at the dime store."

"Do you have any idea what the cops would do if they stopped you and you showed them this toy? Ever heard of 'Shoot first and ask questions later'?"

"That'd be their mistake," Donny said.

"And your funeral." Zach passed the toy gun to Kathleen. "Stick this in your purse."

"Oh, man. That's not fair," Donny complained. "You're not my schoolteacher, Foster."

"But I am your boss. Don't make me kick your sorry butt out of here."

"Okay, okay." He held up his hands in a placating gesture. "So how come you're here?"

"To kick you out." But Zach's expression was kind. "I've got no work today, so everybody gets a day off."

"Cool." Donny bobbed his head up and down. "How about tomorrow?"

"We're busy tomorrow. If you're not working on displays, I'll need help setting up my paintings at the gallery. By the way, you're invited to the opening."

"Cool."

"On the following conditions. You don't steal the food. You don't hit on the women. You dress like a civilized human being. And you don't carry any weapons—toys or otherwise."

Donny rolled his eyes and appealed to Kathleen. "Does he sound like a parent or what?"

"He does," she agreed. "But he's wrong about one thing. The women would probably enjoy being hit upon, if you do it with style."

"No way!" Donny said. "Those society babes?"

"I happen to know several 'babes' who are partial to young men with tattoos."

"Don't encourage him," Foster warned. "Donny, you be polite to everybody at the showing. Got it?"

Glumly, Donny nodded.

"Now let's get out of here."

Donny uttered his catchall "Cool," and opened the door for Kathleen to leave. While Foster turned on the answering machine and locked up, Donny asked her, "Do you really think I could get a date with one of those rich girls?"

"It's possible. But you've got to be polite. Gentlemanly."

"Gentleman Donny." He drew himself up, stuck out his chest, then deflated like a balloon. "My little brother's good at that stuff. Chad's only fifteen, but he's got girls falling all over him."

"Well, you see? It works."

"Not for me." He slunk toward an aged Chevy. "See you around, Ms. Welles."

When Foster herded Kathleen into the van and set out for the golf course, she could tell he was irritated. "What's wrong?" she asked.

"That wasn't good advice you gave to Donny."

"Why not? Cleaned up, he'd be a handsome young man. Any woman would be complimented if he paid attention to her."

He shook his head. "You're wrong."

Feeling an irritation of her own, she asked, "Could you explain?"

"Those 'society babes,' as Donny called them, could not care less about a guy like him. He's got no family heritage. No money. He's not going to Harvard. All he can get from dating one of those girls is hurt and disappointed when she dumps him for a pre-law student."

"Are you saying that all females who come from money are snobs?"

"That's about the size of it."

His reverse discrimination infuriated her. Because he'd come from a rough background, he assumed that all moneyed people were shallow, callous and incapable of true passion. Kathleen felt the heat rising in her cheeks. But she held her tongue. She didn't want to argue. Not today. She would not allow herself to be goaded, even if Foster pushed the issue.

Foster pushed. "Like you and me."

"Excuse me?"

"The princess and the pauper," he said. "You might enjoy a brief flirtation with me, but if it came down to a serious relationship, you'd never follow through. After all, what would your society friends say?"

For the second time, Kathleen was tempted to launch into a serious argument. How dare he assume that he knew the secrets of her heart? He couldn't be more wrong. "Don't blame *me* if *you're* afraid of commitment."

"Me? I'm not afraid."

"You're taking the coward's way out," she continued. "Refusing to try because you might be hurt."

"Listen, Kathleen—"

"No, you listen to me." Her tone was restrained but emphatic. "There might be uncomfortable moments when people who are different embark on a relationship. But only one thing is truly important. Love, Foster. Love is what makes a relationship. Love is the only reason for a commitment."

"That's a very pretty thought. But it's a fairy tale."

"I agree. And we all need fairy tales. Everybody does. Painters and princesses. Professors and plumbers. Scientists and strippers. We all need something to believe in, something to hope for."

"And that something is . . ."

"It's love. You know I'm right about this."

"Do I?"

He'd never dreamed she would be so perceptive. She spoke like a woman who knew the many faces of love. The heartache. The ecstasy. And that surprised him.

From what Zach had seen of Kathleen, he'd presumed she was the sort of willful female who threw small breakable objects when she was angry. He could see her pitching a drink in someone's face, could hear her melodious voice lashing out with the full force of a hurricane wind. But this maturity, this sensitivity he was seeing in her today, made him think he'd misjudged her.

At a stoplight, he glanced toward her. Her face had flushed crimson from her throat to her hairline. A small muscle in her jaw twitched, and her dark eyes flared with righteous indignation. He was tempted to tell her how cute she was when she was angry, but he thought better of it. No point in pushing his luck.

The telephone in her purse rang, and after a brief conversation she informed him, "Helen has set an appointment with Dr. Armitage for my mother at one o'clock. We have to get Dr. Mathers there."

"But it's after eleven. We'll have to get Mathers to come with us right away."

"Yes, we will."

Zach wasn't convinced that they could separate a doctor from his golf game, but the determined expression on Kathleen's face told him otherwise. He pulled into the parking lot, and she raced inside the country club, a handsome brick building that resembled an English country house. She reappeared in a flash, running to the van.

"We're in luck," she said, jumping into the passenger seat. "He's on the back nine, and there's a road that comes close."

Following her directions through the wealthy residential area that bordered much of the golf course, Zach ended up parking his van on a dead-end road that led to a wooded area and a gully. "You know your way around out here?"

"My family belongs to this club. I used to caddy for my father." She hopped from the van. "Hurry, Foster."

Surefooted and fleet, Kathleen slung her purse over her shoulder and crossed the gully, easily leaping the narrow creek that trickled through its center. In her light sundress, she was graceful as a wood nymph, Zach thought. Her slender legs propelled her quickly. Her new haircut swung smoothly as she led the way.

Through a thicket of pine trees and shrubbery, they emerged on the manicured fairway. The overwhelming vision of emerald everywhere deserved a moment's appreciation, but Kathleen did not hesitate. She loped along the line of the trees. Zach had to sprint to overtake her.

"Hold it!"

He caught her arm, and she spun around. Breathless with exertion, she gasped, "What is it?"

"It's a big course," he said. "How are we going to search the whole thing?"

"The guy in the pro shop keeps track of which foursome is where so he can schedule. He told me that Dr. Mathers and his party are either at this hole or the next."

On the green at the fourteenth hole, Kathleen let out a cry of relief. "There he is! I recognize those godawful turquoise trousers. Honestly, I will never understand why men wear such horrid outfits to play golf."

She ran to the edge of the green and waited while one of the foursome sank a six-foot putt. Then Kathleen was on Dr. Mathers like a flea on a dog. She tapped his shoulder. "You have to come with me, Dr. Mathers. This is an emergency."

A middle-aged man with thick eyebrows and thinning brown hair stared down at her. Zach thought he had an interesting chin. Very strong, with a dimple creasing the center. Zach would have liked to paint that face. Mathers was obviously annoyed at Kathleen's pesky interruption. His pale eyes glared. But he was also concerned.

"Do I know you, young lady?" Mathers asked.

"Come with me, please," she said. "My mother needs you. I can't explain right now, but she needs your diagnostic help."

"Is your mother one of my patients?"

"She will be. Please, Doctor."

"Who is her current physician?"

"Armitage," Kathleen said. "She has a one o'clock appointment with him, but she needs a specialist. She needs you."

Mathers asked his three companions to excuse him and stepped aside to confer with Kathleen. In Zach's opinion, the doctor showed remarkable tact and understanding. "Young lady, I can't march into Dr. Armitage's office and demand to see someone he is treating. Much as I appreciate your faith in me, I don't believe I can help you."

"My name is Kathleen Welles. My mother is Hannah Welles."

"I'm sorry," he said.

Kathleen searched her memory for a detail that would convince him. After her mother had her stroke, she'd become so well acquainted with Dr. Mathers that she knew the birthday of his three children and his wife. She knew that he was a collector. He loved fine art. "The Degas," she said. "If you come with me, it's yours."

During one of Dr. Mathers's house calls, he'd admired a small Degas sculpture of a ballet dancer at Hannah's home. After consulting with her mother, Kathleen had made a gift of the piece. "The statue is about twelve inches high. Bronze. A dancer *en pointe.*"

His eyebrows rose, creasing his tanned forehead. "Strange," he said. "I'm not familiar with such a sculpture, but the moment you mentioned it, I had a very sharp mental image."

"I know this is unusual, Doctor, but I have solid reasons for believing that you are the only person who can really help my mother. You have to come with me."

"Absolutely not. Now please excuse me."

"You and I will know each other very well during the coming year. I'll come to your daughter's birthday party in September and bring her a hat that she'll wear every day. I'll help your wife shop for the Alaska cruise that you're planning to take in August."

"How did you know about the cruise?"

She couldn't tell him that the cruise had already happened, couldn't explain that he and his wife had had a marvelous time. "Come with me, and I'll tell you."

He turned toward Foster. "Can you explain what's going on here?"

"Me?" Zach straightened his shoulders.

"This young lady seems . . . disturbed."

"She knows what she's doing," Zach replied. His opinion of the good doctor lowered several notches. "This isn't a joke, Doc. It's real important to Kathleen that you see her mother."

"I'm sorry, but I can't. It would be highly improper for me to interfere."

"Ethics be damned," Kathleen said. She kept her voice low, but Zach could hear her desperation as she pleaded, "Please, Doctor. We're talking about my mother's life."

"I'm sure Dr. Armitage can handle the situation."

Kathleen let out a frantic gasp that nearly broke Zach's heart. She was trying so hard. Didn't this jerk doctor understand?

Mathers turned away. "Now if you'll excuse me, I have a golf game to finish, and I'm one under par."

"Under par is right," Zach muttered. Before he could consider the wisdom of his actions, he reached into Kathleen's purse and grasped Donny's toy pistol in his hand. He held on to Mathers's arm and jammed the butt into the doctor's rib cage. "You're coming with us, Doctor. Now."

Kathleen stepped up beside him. In a low voice, she said, "I'm sorry it came to this, but you'd better listen to him."

"Call him off, Miss Welles."

"I won't let my mother suffer needlessly because you're playing a game of golf. Tell your friends that you've been called away on a medical emergency."

Zach dug the plastic gun in deeper. He called on his past, his street smarts. It didn't take much to make his voice sound dangerous. "Do what she says. I don't like people like you. Never have. It wouldn't break my heart to pull this trigger."

"You wouldn't dare." Mathers stared into his eyes.

Zach looked back, unwavering and cool, though his adrenaline was pumping hard. Too well he remembered this edge, this dangerous line between rage and violence. He'd never backed away from a fight in his life. "Try me."

Mathers was convinced. "Okay, just calm down. I'll do whatever you say. Just be careful." He waved to the other three in the golf foursome. "Sorry, guys. I've got to go."

"It's an emergency," Kathleen called out. "We'll have to take your golf cart."

There were mutters of complaint, but the other three men agreed. Who could argue with a medical emergency?

Without removing the gun from Mathers's side, Zach told Kathleen to grab the good doctor's golf clubs. "Move it, Doctor. We're parked on the other side of the gully."

Kathleen jumped behind the wheel of the golf cart, and they careered over the rolling green hills. When they were out of sight of the threesome, Kathleen took a deep breath. She didn't quite believe that they'd done such a thing. Kidnapping a doctor. Zipping off in a getaway golf cart. "I'm sorry, Doctor. I had hoped this would be easier."

"So did I."

At the gully, they abandoned the cart. Zach said to Kathleen, "You'd better turn on the charm, princess. That doctor could press charges."

She hissed. "So? It's a fake gun."

"When it comes to threatening people at gunpoint—fake or real—there are laws, Kathleen." He climbed the slight incline behind Dr. Mathers. "I can't believe we did that."

"We're a regular Bonnie and Clyde."

He gave her arm a squeeze. "I don't quite know how to tell you this, Kathleen. You've never been on the wrong side of the law. But abducting a doctor isn't a joke."

"After he sees my mother, everything will be fine."

"There's another thought," he complained. "Your mother. What's she going to think when we march a specialist into her appointment at gunpoint?"

"She'll be glad I brought him when he saves her life. The result is what's important." Uncharacteristically, she added, "Besides, I don't care a damn for appearances. Give me the gun, Foster. You have to drive."

She herded Dr. Mathers into the back of the van and turned around in the passenger seat to keep an eye on him. A year in the future, she'd have plenty of time to think about her actions. But right now? She was too desperate to care.

Chapter Seven

At one-fifteen, in the waiting room of Dr. Armitage, Kathleen breezed past the receptionist. Her hostage, Dr. Gregory Mathers, preceded her. His angry glower was enough to repel the nurses as he marched stiff legged into the clean, narrow hallway lined on one side with numbered examination rooms.

"Mother?" Kathleen called out. "Hannah?"

"Kathleen?" The response came from examining room number three. "Kathleen? Is that you?"

"Let's go, Doc." Behind her, Kathleen heard Foster arguing with one of the nurses, but she didn't stop to see what he was doing to distract them. She followed Mathers into the small room where her mother perched on an examining table, still dressed in her street clothes with her suit jacket removed.

"Kathleen? What are you doing here? Who is this man?"

"Dr. Gregory Mathers," she said triumphantly. "He's going to examine you."

Hannah's dark-eyed gaze flitted back and forth between them. Clearly annoyed, she snapped, "Isn't it enough that I made this appointment? What else will you demand?"

"Mother, I'm sorry. But I'm doing what's best for you. Really." Kathleen couldn't bring herself to repeat the words that were becoming second nature to her: *Trust me.* Her behavior, she knew, was more than odd. Borderline criminal, to tell the truth. But what choice did she have? The fates had not chosen to cooperate, and Kathleen would not allow herself to be beaten. No measure was too extreme.

She was grateful to Foster for taking charge on the golf course when she'd been on the verge of despair. They worked well as a team, she thought. He was the brawn; she was the brains. Inadvertently, she smiled, not paying the slightest attention as her mother continued her complaints in a rising tone of voice. Kathleen tuned out Hannah, the examining room and the stormy presence of Dr. Mathers. She allowed her mind to be consumed by the image of Zachary Foster. He was muscular, masculine, forgivably macho. And so much more...

Dr. Armitage slipped into the room and closed the door. With four people inside, the space was cramped to the point of claustrophobia. Only Armitage seemed not to mind. Calmly, he sat beside Hannah and gently patted her hand. Kathleen recalled the gesture; after her mother's stroke, when Hannah was in the hospital near death, Armitage had blamed himself and quietly wept at her bedside.

Kathleen shook away the dark memory. That wasn't going to happen. Not now. There would be no blame, no guilt, no sorrow. Her mother would be all right. Cheerfully, she said, "Hello, Dr. Armitage."

He nodded toward Mathers and frowned at her. "What exactly are you doing, Kathleen? How did you get this old sinner off the golf course on a Thursday?"

"With this." Kathleen brandished the pistol.

"Oh, my Lord," her mother said. "Have you completely lost your mind?"

Kathleen placed the weapon in Dr. Mathers's hand. "It's only a toy, but my intention is serious. Deadly serious. Though I respect Dr. Armitage, I want a second opinion, the opinion of a specialist. Unless the two of you can prevent it, my mother will have a devastating stroke at four-fifteen this afternoon."

Dr. Mathers took two steps to the trash can and hurled the plastic pistol into it with shattering force. He pivoted to confront Kathleen. "Miss Welles, you may rest assured that I fully intend to prosecute you and your accomplice."

She bit her lip, not knowing what to say. He was perfectly justified in his complaint.

Her mother groaned. "What have you done?"

Mathers faced her. "She interrupted my golf game when I was one under par. She and her boyfriend, a rough-looking character, abducted me."

"Foster," her mother surmised. "I knew he was no good."

"Then," Mathers continued, "they hijacked a golf cart."

"I apologize," Kathleen said.

"Get out of this room," he snarled. "I don't want to hear your voice. I don't want to see your face."

"But will you—"

"As long as I'm here and my day is ruined, Dr. Armitage and I will examine your mother. I assume, since this poor woman has spent years dealing with you as a daughter, her stress levels are sky-high."

"Thank you so much!" Kathleen bubbled, ignoring the insult. "Dr. Armitage, Dr. Mathers, thank you. I appreciate—"

"Get out!" Mathers roared.

"Bye, Mom. I'll be outside."

She crept down the hallway, past the nurses' office. Kathleen should have been ashamed of her behavior. Instead, she was jubilant. She'd done it! Gotten her mother an examination with a man who could help her.

She sauntered into the waiting room. There were only three people seated in the spacious area. A man with a dreadful sniffle. A tall, athletic-looking woman. And Zachary Foster. He'd centered himself on a long, forest green sofa, where he sat hunched over, reading a dog-eared issue of *Reader's Digest*. Kathleen bounded across the room and sat down beside him.

"This is it, Foster. I've done everything I can. Now it's up to the doctors."

"Congratulations."

She kissed his cheek. "I couldn't have done it without you."

He groaned. "Don't remind me, okay?"

"But it was brilliant. Did you see the expression on Mathers's face when we—"

"We're not going to talk about it. Besides, I've got to ask you about something else." He kept his voice low in deference to the other people waiting. "Why are you so certain about what's going to happen today? Why do you believe your mother is going to have a stroke? When I saw her this morning, she looked healthier and more fit than most women half her age."

"She covers her infirmities well," Kathleen hedged. "For years now, her blood pressure has been rising. I've been worried about her."

"That's not the whole truth. You had details. You said the stroke would happen at four-fifteen, down to the minute. Why? And where did you get the information about Mathers's family?"

"Lucky guess?"

"Knowing about his daughter's birthday and a cruise to Alaska are more than coincidence."

The frantic effort of bringing Dr. Mathers to this office caught up with her. She was tired, too exhausted to come up with a creative excuse. Her shoulders rose and fell in a shrug.

"From the fortune-teller?" he asked.

"In a way." She stared down at her hands, her fingers knotting in her lap. She was much too tired to lie. "Please don't ask me about this right now, Foster."

"But—"

"You don't want to discuss kidnapping the doctor, and I don't want to talk about this."

He cupped her chin and turned her face toward him so she couldn't avoid his gaze. "A while ago, you asked me to trust you."

She peered into his eyes, mesmerized by their blue intensity.

"I do," he said. "God help me, I do trust you. I don't know what the hell is going on. I don't know why I'm having visions of hourglasses or why the painted hands on a clock moved. But I trust you, Kathleen. I believe in you."

Unmindful of the other people, she collapsed into the shelter of his arms, leaning against his strong, well-muscled chest. He believed in her. Half her battle was over. The race Mrs. van Winkle had described was almost won. And Kathleen would succeed in changing the future by reliving the past.

Foster whispered into her hair, "But that is definitely the last time I'm going to kidnap a doctor and steal a golf cart for you."

"But what if I have another princess demand? Fetch me the moon and the stars."

"No way."

"Slay me a dragon? Fetch the magical toad?"

"Stop," he said. "My grandmother warned me about princesses like you."

"You'd dare to refuse?" she teased. "Even if I commanded you?"

"For sure, I'd refuse if you commanded." He stroked her hair, his strong, sensitive fingers tangling in the strands. "But if you asked me real nice, I'd probably go along with you."

"Why?" she whispered, hoping she'd hear words of love and commitment.

"I don't know, princess. Maybe I'm as crazy as you are."

Oh, well. For now, snuggled in the crook of his arm, she felt safe and content. They had shared a remarkable morning, and the dinner she had planned for the early evening would be the perfect prelude to love. Then the day would truly be a conquest. She would have repaired all the horrible mistakes she'd made the first time around.

Her tension ebbed, and she allowed herself to relax for a moment. She must have dozed, because the next thing she realized, Dr. Armitage was standing before her. "Kathleen, please come into my office."

"What time is it?" she asked, struggling toward alertness.

Foster consulted his pocket watch. "Two-fifteen."

"Is my mother all right?"

"She'll be fine." Dr. Armitage smiled, but the expression in his kindly eyes was grave. "Come with me."

She rose to her feet and linked hands with Foster. "I need you," she said. "I don't think this is good news."

Dr. Armitage's office was tastefully arrayed with the requisite medical texts and framed diplomas. Kathleen perched anxiously on the edge of a leather chair. Foster stood behind her, as if he was her protector, ready to ward off any threat. Not that there was any apparent danger from the good-hearted doctor who settled in behind the desk and folded his arms across his slight paunch. "I've admitted your mother to Mercy Hospital across the street," he said.

Kathleen tensed.

"Don't worry," he said. "It's only for a few days of observation and testing."

"Thank God," she breathed. It was the best she could hope for. "Can you tell me more?"

"Her condition is good. This is merely routine, a precaution to explore her symptoms." He paused. "You were right, Kathleen. According to some preliminary tests, it was very possible that your mother could have been in deep trouble. Her blood pressure was astronomical, and at her age . . ."

"But now? She'll be okay?"

"Dr. Mathers believes the crisis can be averted." He shifted uncomfortably in his chair. "You were right about that, too. Calling in Mathers to consult." He frowned, unhappy with himself. "Yes, indeed, you were right. I don't have his expertise. In a routine physical exam, I might have missed the signs of immediate danger, might have sent your mother on her way with a new prescription and a promise to contact her with test results in a few days."

Dr. Mathers burst into the room. He was energized, pacing back and forth, rubbing his high forehead.

"Speak of the devil," Armitage said.

"I'd rather speak to this little witch." He glared at Kathleen. "Are you prescient? Did you have a vision, Miss Welles? Did you use a magic potion or tarot cards? Dammit, woman, how on earth did you know your mother was a candidate for a stroke?"

"Gosh, you know," she hedged. "I'm not sure. She just didn't seem well."

"I'm not buying, it," he said. "You told me she'd have a stroke today. At four-fifteen. That's not the kind of casual observation made by a layperson."

"She's my mother. I had a sense that—"

"No." He stopped in front of her chair and leaned down to look her straight in the eye. "The witches in Salem, Massachusetts, were burned for less. How did you know?"

"Back off," Zach said. He stepped around her chair to confront the doctor. "Maybe the next time somebody tells you there's an emergency, you'll listen."

"How did she know?" he asked Foster. "You're better acquainted with her than I am. Maybe you have some idea what she's up to."

"It's not important," Foster said.

"If she's got some kind of diagnostic tool, I want to know about it."

"Come off it, Doc." He squared off with Mathers. "Kathleen is no scientist. You're not going to get any profound answers by badgering her."

"Don't you tell me how to do my job."

"Your job is healing," Zach said.

"Amen," said Dr. Armitage. "You know, Mathers, he's right. Sometimes we doctors forget there are forces beyond our control. We forget that the power of prayer can be more effective than all our training and medical knowledge."

Though he had the good grace to appear somewhat abashed, Mathers was far from calmed down. He pointed at Kathleen and Foster. "Neither of you is off the hook. Understand? I'm not going to forget that you kidnapped me."

"Yeah?" Zach cocked his chin. His hands were loosely fisted at his sides. His street-fighter posture betrayed his roots, and Kathleen was glad to be with a man who could protect her from bullies.

Zach's voice was dangerously low. "Let me tell you something, Doc. If you go public with this story, you'll look bad. Real bad. People won't like to hear about a doctor who had to be dragged from his country-club golf course at gunpoint so he could save a woman's life."

"What you did was wrong," Mathers said.

"I'm not saying it was a good move. But Kathleen was desperate to have your help."

She rose gracefully from her chair. "There's no more to be said, except to thank you both. I'll see my mother before I leave, and I'll be in touch concerning her condition."

Placing her hand on Foster's arm, they left the office and marched through the waiting area, their heads held high. When they were in the hallway outside the offices, she laughed out loud. "You were great!"

"No, Kathleen," he said softly, "you're the one who deserves congratulations. Nobody believed you. But you saved your mother's life."

She could feel herself blushing again. "Anybody else would have done the same."

"I doubt that." He held her shoulders. "You're pretty great yourself, princess."

In his voice, she heard praise. In his eyes, she saw admiration. Kathleen tilted up her chin, and he lightly kissed her mouth. A whisper of a kiss. She closed her eyes, imagining more.

Foster must have read her mind, because he slipped one hand behind the nape of her neck and held her while he tasted more deeply. His tongue parted her lips and thrust inside. The taste of him—hot, slick, hungry—aroused her. She pressed against him, and for a timeless moment they were joined.

She sighed when they separated, and she looked up at him. He was the most handsome man she'd ever seen. His hair, his brow, his blue eyes, the rugged planes of his face. And he was by far the most dear. "Foster," she murmured. "Zachary Emile Foster."

If only she could claim him for her own. For all time.

"Let's go see your mom," he said. "Correction. You see her. I don't think she's quite ready for me. I'll wait outside."

"Good plan."

At Mercy Hospital, Kathleen slashed through the red tape with remarkable alacrity, calling upon her experience with hospital bureaucracy during the year her mother was ill. In moments she'd found the critical-care unit and, after giving Foster's hand a fond squeeze, was inside a restricted glass-walled room. "Hello, Mom."

"I didn't even know I was sick." Hannah was sitting in bed, surrounded by a variety of monitors and machines. Her street clothing had been discarded, and she wore a simple hospital-issue cotton gown. "This is most inconvenient. I'm not prepared for a hospital stay."

Kathleen had the antidote in her purse. She pulled out the cellular phone and dialed her mother's secretary. "Helen, my mother is going to be in the hospital for a few days. Anything that is not an absolute emergency can be put on hold until after the weekend."

"In the hospital," Helen said. There was a frightened quaver in her voice, but she recovered immediately. "Mercy Hospital?"

"Yes, she'll be here for a few days of testing and observation, and she would prefer that you not make any general announcements." Kathleen looked toward her mother for confirmation, and Hannah nodded.

"There's nothing on her desk that can't wait," Helen said. "But by Monday, some documents will need reviewing, some contracts will need to be signed. I'll take care of payroll and payment orders. But my authority is limited, Kathleen. I'm afraid you'll be required to take over your mother's duties for a while."

"Monday morning," Kathleen promised. She vividly recalled how she'd felt a year ago, when she became acting president of Welles, Incorporated. Dread. Confusion. Intense fear of failure. This time, the responsibilities seemed like second nature.

When she issued directives to Helen, the words came easily. And Kathleen realized that this part of the future had not changed. Though her mother would not be incapacitated, Kathleen would take over her job. Just as she had done before. She would grow up, become an adult. And she was grateful to shed the mantle of princess.

Helen wished her good luck. "You'll need it."

"Oh, and Helen, if it's not too much trouble, would you drop by the house and pick up some appropriate clothing and toiletries for Hannah's hospital stay? There's a blue nightgown and matching robe. Estée Lauder face cream. Blow-dryer. Toothbrush." Kathleen listed everything she could think of, ending with, "And, of course, Obsession perfume."

She glanced toward Hannah. "Anything else?"

"The book on my nightstand. A couple of magazines."

Kathleen relayed the message and told Helen how to reach Hannah at the hospital, then turned back to her mother. "Can you think of anything else you need?"

"Dom Pérignon and a catered dinner from Cliff Young's." She scowled. "I haven't eaten hospital food since you were born, and I can still remember the heartburn."

Into the telephone, Kathleen said, "I think we've covered everything, Helen."

"I suppose I should thank you," her mother said. "That doctor you dragged in said I was in imminent danger. There's some kind of blockage or irregularity or something. I don't know."

Kathleen leaned across the bed. "You listen to the doctors and the nurses. Don't even think about pulling any kind of stunts like ordering in dinner. Okay?"

"But I don't feel all that bad."

Her mother's hand lay still and pale on the sheets. The fragile bones and tendons stood out through the translucent skin, reminding Kathleen how ephemeral life could be. So brief. Then, in a flash, gone. Transformed into eternal time bubbles. She gently held her mother's hand and gave it a squeeze.

"I'm so lucky," Kathleen said. This time, she had the chance to say all the important words that were so often left unspoken when someone was suddenly ill. "I want to apologize, Mother, for all the times I caused you grief." Tears rose up behind her eyelids. "I haven't always been a good daughter, and, many times, I've hurt you. For those times, I am truly sorry."

Hannah cleared her throat. When Kathleen looked into her face, she saw that her mother was also on the verge of crying. "Well, dear, does this mean you'll do exactly as I say from this moment forward?"

"You know me better than that."

"Yes, I do."

"I love you very much, Mom. Take care of yourself, and do everything the doctors tell you. It's so important to me that you recover your health and continue to live a strong, productive life."

"It would be easier if I had grandchildren."

Kathleen grinned. "You never give up, do you?"

"Stubbornness runs in the family, my darling child."

A white-coated lab technician appeared in the door. "Sorry to interrupt," she said, "but I need to draw some blood."

Kathleen went toward the door. "I'll see you tomorrow, Mom."

Outside, she walked slowly down the antiseptic hospital hallway. Kathleen cherished the warmth inside her, the sweet feeling of love. In the years since her father and brother died, the rift between mother and daughter had grown wide and deep and seemingly impassable. Now there was a bridge.

Only one more treacherous journey faced her. The argument with Foster.

Until now, the sequence of events for this day differed from the previous time she'd endured these twenty-four hours. The last time, she'd been bored and lazy. Fretting over small disappointments. This time, she'd been racing to beat the clock.

But now, it was almost three in the afternoon. That was precisely the time she'd gone to Foster's studio and seen the paintings.

Kathleen wasn't sure if that was a good or a bad omen.

The special dinner she'd planned was at five. She still needed to shower, wash her hair, dress and perfume herself. She had to be the most seductive creature on the face of the earth. Two hours wasn't nearly enough time. But when she saw Foster in the waiting room, gazing out the window toward the nearby park, two hours felt much too long to wait.

The light from outdoors seemed to glow on his cheekbones. His expression was pensive, thoughtful.

"A penny for them," she said.

"Your Mom's okay?"

"She's getting the best care I could ever hope for." She dug in her purse, pulled out a shiny penny and tossed it to him. "What else are you thinking about?"

"You," he said.

A smile rushed to her face. "What about me?"

"There's something I want to do to that portrait of you. Let's zip down to the gallery so you can pick up your car. Then come to my studio."

Her brief sojourn into bliss ended with a crash. His studio was the last place on earth she wanted to be. That was the place she'd destroyed their budding relationship.

She reminded herself that it didn't have to be the same as it was last time. With her frantic efforts, she'd changed her mother's destiny. That should give her confidence. Things weren't the same as before. She had a clean start, a fresh canvas, so to speak.

Still, Kathleen preferred not to tempt fate. She didn't want to deal with the problem of the portraits until she was sure Zachary Foster loved her. Later, she would know. Much later.

Lightly, she asked, "You haven't forgotten about our dinner, have you?"

"Of course not," he said.

"Well, I'd like to get ready. Why don't we pick up my car, then—after dinner—we'll go to your studio."

"I want to take care of this right now." He winked. "Besides, I have a surprise for you."

"A surprise?" Her blood ran cold.

He eyed her suspiciously. "Is something wrong?"

"No, nothing." Not yet.

"Okay, then stop by my studio. This will only take a minute, Kathleen."

Unfortunately, minutes were all she had.

Chapter Eight

After picking up her BMW at the gallery, Kathleen drove slowly through the Capitol Hill streets toward Foster's studio, knowing where she was going but not wanting to arrive.

Severe trepidation was her companion. There could be only one reason he wanted her to come to the studio. He'd used the same words the last time she'd lived this day. *A surprise!* A terrible surprise, she thought, as awful as opening Pandora's box and unleashing pestilence and sorrow upon the world.

But then, she remembered, there was hope. The last entity to be released from Pandora's box was hope.

Kathleen clung to that thought. Hope. After all, this time she would not be taken by surprise. Surely, this time she would react more rationally.

As she drove nearer and nearer, her tension increased. She circled the block twice before entering the alley and parking behind Foster's van.

He opened the door to his carriage house and leaned against the door frame. "What's the secret password?"

The same words! She was dumbfounded, unable to speak.

"Come on, Kathleen, nobody enters my kingdom without a password."

"Pandora," she whispered. "Hope."

This time, when she tried to sidle past him, he dropped his arm, blocking her path. "Halt."

"I gave you a password," she said.

He coiled his arm around her and pulled her inside. "But you didn't give me a kiss."

This time *was* different! Gratefully, she embraced him. When their lips met, she kissed him fiercely, purposefully. She willed him to care about her, to love her as she loved him, to understand.

His body reacted. His hands stroked the fabric of her light sundress, caressing, pulling her against his arousal.

When she leaned her head back, her lips parted. She was panting, gasping. He fitted her body exactly to his. Wonderful, she thought, he felt so wonderful. So very masculine, so very right. She longed for their clothing to melt away, for their bodies to become as one. Now was the right time. Now, this minute, she wanted to make love. A love that would last forever.

"Kathleen," he said, "we have to stop."

"Please, don't."

"If I don't stop now," he warned, "I won't be able to."

Sweet assent was on the tip of her tongue. *Yes,* she wanted to say. *Yes, make love to me now.* She ached with the need for him. Her breasts felt heavy. Her nipples were painfully sensitive. An unceasing throbbing echoed in her loins. "Don't stop."

"What about dinner?"

"Don't care." She wanted him now... before anything terrible happened.

"What about my surprise?" He swept her hair off her forehead and kissed her brow, then the tip of her nose.

She stood waiting with her eyelids closed for him to taste her mouth once again. But his embrace loosened, and he patted her bottom. "Why don't you slip behind the screen and take off your clothes?"

"What?"

"Well, I was going to show you the portrait and the two smaller studies, but there's something not quite right about one of them. A couple of brush strokes."

"I don't understand."

"I want you to pose, Kathleen."

She'd just offered herself to him, and he was thinking about his art. She groaned with frustration. When would this waiting be over? "We don't have time for posing," she objected. "I've planned dinner."

"And I'm sure it's going to be great." He was guiding her through the airy studio. "This won't take more than half an hour."

Reluctantly, she went behind the black-and-white art-deco screen. Her breath came in shallow puffs. She folded her arms beneath her breasts and held on tight. Why was he doing this to her? Why was he torturing her this way?

Because he doesn't know, she told herself. He doesn't know that the last time she lived this day, they had fought, and she'd lashed out and destroyed his work.

"Come on, Kathleen. Hurry up."

"Wait a minute." During the time she'd spent posing, Kathleen had learned a little bit about his craft. If he intended to work on one of the paintings, it would take time to dry. Which must mean that he didn't intend to display the picture at the gallery showing. He must have made that decision.

With all her might, she hoped and prayed that her conclusion was right and Foster had decided on his own that showing the portraits would be an invasion of her privacy. It made sense. After the experiences of this day, they knew each other more deeply. Maybe he did understand her. Maybe Foster truly was a living, breathing embodiment of that totally unique, almost mythical creature she believed him to be: a sensitive yet masculine man.

Hope, she remembered. Pandora's hope.

Stripped to her bra and panties, she wrapped herself in a light cotton robe and came out from behind the screen. The painting on his working easel was the smallest of the three.

"Sit over there, Kathleen, on the futon."

Her posture was prim, knees together and arms folded beneath her breasts. A year ago, when she'd posed for him, she'd had two months to make herself feel comfortable about being nearly nude. Now she felt shy.

Without a word, he stretched her legs out. His manner was businesslike, not at all sexual. He was Zachary Foster, artist. And she was his model, the object he would paint.

"Lean your head back and look up," he instructed. He arranged her arms, stepped back, scrutinized her position and shook his head. "Not quite right. Slip the robe off the upper part of your body."

Her pulse quickened. Had she really been able to do this before without becoming aroused? She lowered the robe from her shoulders.

He arranged her again. His hands left hot imprints on her flesh as he tilted her chin up and arranged her so that she was braced on one arm.

"There," he said, and she heard the satisfaction in his voice. "Is that comfortable? Can you hold it for ten minutes?"

"I think so."

He slipped a CD into his sound system, and she heard the wail of a saxophone, the same tape he'd been listening to last night.

"Two tracks," he said. "That's all the time it'll take."

"Okay."

"Maybe it's your hair, after all," he said as he went behind the easel. "You have a different look, more of an edge."

"An edge?" What did that mean?

"Kathleen, please don't talk. Just sit there. Don't move, and I can do this quickly."

She kept herself still, her neck back and her eyes gazing up at the skylight, through which she could see fluffy white clouds drifting in a sky of purest azure. While the jazz saxophone wept, she gradually became aware of every muscle in her body. She wanted to yawn, to stretch, to move. A prickling sensation, like that of a thousand tiny pins, went up and down her arm. Her jaw clenched. Sitting immobile was incredibly hard work.

"Relax," he ordered.

After the first cut on the tape ended, she had entered a state that was not unlike meditation. Conscious thought was suspended as she floated, seemingly detached from her body. There was no time, no space. Only the moment. She existed only in this moment.

Then he was right beside her. "Don't move. I'm going to do something we tried once before."

The tips of his fingers deftly unfastened the front clasp of her brassiere, and he swept aside the flimsy bit of lace.

Though his behavior was utterly professional, not at all sexual, she felt incredibly excited. Wanton and free.

"One more track," he said. "Just one more."

He was back at his easel. Though she could not see him, Kathleen sensed that he was working furiously, daubing at the colors on his palette, mixing and preparing to attain exactly the right hue. When she'd been able to watch him paint, his intensity amazed her. His strong hands became an extension of his whole manly posture. His legs were braced apart, his broad shoulders hunched with his concentration. His bold, sure brush strokes expressed a masculine vigor.

"Foster, I can't hold this much longer."

"A minute. Only a minute."

She counted her breaths, listened to her pulse. Breathe. Breathe.

And then he was beside her again. Gently, he lowered her on the futon. Her gaze drifted slowly from the skylight. From the blue of the skies to the blue of his eyes.

"You're very beautiful, Kathleen. The best model I've ever had."

"Better than the models in New York? In Paris?"

"New York. Paris. San Francisco. Milan. I had to travel around the world to realize that the most beautiful woman was right here in Denver, my hometown."

A dangerous conversation, she remembered. These words had been spoken before. Was she powerless to stop fate?

Not at all! she chided herself. Once today, she'd changed the course of destiny. She'd saved her mother a year of suffering. She must be able to do the same for herself. She must.

But she couldn't think. She could only stare at the man she loved. He was so handsome, so dear. His smile thrilled her to the depths of her being.

"I like to paint you," he said.

He took a thick, clean camel-hair brush from behind his ear and lightly stroked her forehead, then tickled below her chin.

"You . . . you've never done this before."

"I'm a man, princess. I have only so much willpower. I've looked at your body for hours, studied it. I want to see how that satin skin feels. I want to feel you moving against me." With the brush, he continued to stroke her.

"Foster . . ." she protested weakly, dazed and aroused.

"Lie still."

"But . . ."

"Lie very still, and be silent."

Her gaze locked with his. And his brush trailed down her throat.

"Close your eyes." His blue-eyed gaze melted her resolve. "Princess, do as I say."

She lay before him, exposed and vulnerable, powerless to refuse him anything. Her eyelids shut, and, without sight, her other senses seemed magnified. The saxophone grew louder, more throbbing. Through the odor of turpentine and oil, she could smell Foster's scent as she felt him moving closer to her. He kissed her lightly. His tongue parted her lips, and the taste of him was excruciatingly sweet.

Using his brush, he drew a wispy circle around one breast, then a smaller circle. When the camel hair touched her bare nipple, Kathleen could not suppress a shudder of pure pleasure. All the sensations she'd held in check for so long flowed through her body like a strong, raging river. And she abandoned herself to the moment.

As he teased her breasts and dragged the feathery brush down her torso, she wriggled with sheer delight.

"Don't move," he said. His voice was husky.

The brush stroked the insides of her thighs. And when it flicked against her silk panties, teasing the most private part of her anatomy, Kathleen gasped.

"Be still," he said.

"No." Her eyes opened. She pulled him into her arms, down upon her on the futon. They kissed with a passion unequaled in her experience. As if starved for contact, they caressed each other, seeking fulfillment for the wondrous ache of desire.

But when she reached for his belt, Foster caught hold of her hand. "God, I want to make love to you." His breathing was ragged. "I've never wanted a woman more in my life."

"Yes," she breathed. "Oh, yes."

"But we've got to talk." His fingers clutched hers. She could feel his power, his strength, the intensity of his struggle. "Can't take advantage. Unprofessional. Dammit, Kathleen, an artist doesn't . . ."

"Doesn't what?"

"We can't."

He sat up straight, then stood. Catching her hands, he pulled her to a sitting posture, then wrapped the robe around her shoulders, covering her nakedness. He stepped away from her and exhaled. "Not yet, my darling Kathleen. First, I have to show you my surprise."

A terrible frustration swept through her, and she wanted to sob. Her shoulders fell, and she drew within herself. His surprise? If she lost him now . . .

Now she knew what Mrs. van Winkle had meant when she spoke of a race so nearly won. If she lost him now, she would surely die. Without him, there would be no reason to go on living. Because the rest of her life would be alone. No other man could take his place. No other lover would suffice.

He set two covered easels opposite the futon. The third, the smallest, was the one he had just been working on. As he prepared to turn it around so she could see, Kathleen was galvanized into action.

She bolted to her feet. "Stop right there, Foster." Still flushed with arousal and half-naked, she could not face those paintings and all they represented. "I have to get dressed."

Before he could reply, she darted behind the screen. Kathleen tossed off the robe, fastened her bra over her throbbing breasts. This emotional state was dangerous, uncontrolled. And she needed to be rational.

A simple plan took shape in her mind. She simply would not see those paintings. She would avoid their argument altogether.

But that was absurd. This day was not the end of time. If she didn't face it today, he might inflict his damned surprise upon her tomorrow, whenever that was. And Kathleen would not be able to predict the events. She would be back into her future life, one year from today. Then she would have no control over what happened.

At least, she thought, she could put off seeing the paintings until after their dinner tonight, after she'd fully seduced him. With that idea, she slipped her sundress over her head and pulled herself together.

She started talking before she came around the screen. "Foster, I don't have time for your surprise right now. We'll have to do it later." She stepped into the studio. "I'm running late, and I have a million things to—"

He'd already unveiled the portraits. She could not avoid them. She tried to avert her gaze, but she could not look away. The portraits had haunted her dreams for a full year. Were they really as good as she remembered?

She was compelled to look.

"Beautiful," she whispered. She had destroyed these pictures, torn them to shreds. She must have been insane! They were so obviously masterpieces. "Oh, Foster, these are magnificent."

"My best work," he said. "This is it, Kathleen. Who knows if I'll ever do anything this perfect again."

She viewed the full-length nude. The large square canvas highlighted the slenderness of the figure, Kathleen's body, standing at ease and yet seeming to be in motion. Her long hair swirled with life, as wonderful as an ocean tide. Visual echoes of her curves resonated across the canvas, creating depth and mystery.

The second picture focused on her torso, leading the eye deeper until the skin and flesh seemed transparent and her naked heart was revealed. Though this portrait was somehow even more erotic, it was slightly less dangerous in that, with her head downturned, only her forehead and closed eyelids were visible. No one could definitely name Kathleen Welles as the model for this picture. The subject was form and shape, the embodiment of woman, not specific to any one person. It might be possible, she thought, to display this painting with no one knowing she had posed for him.

Not so with the smallest of the three canvases. Here he had caught her personality as well as her features. The slight changes he'd made only moments ago enhanced the resemblance. He had added a year. In her eyes, she saw the shadow of sorrow. In the tension of her throat, there was stress and a painful poignancy.

"You know me so well," she said. "You know my heart, my dreams."

"You're an amazing model, Kathleen. I only painted what I saw. You shared yourself with me." He spoke the words she dreaded most in the world. "I'd like to show these works at the gallery."

"But—but you were just working on this one," she said. "It won't be dry."

"Sure it will. I was using acrylic, not oil."

Of course, she thought. Damn. He'd used quick-drying paint for his last touches.

"But you know me," she repeated. "My inner-most feelings. You do, don't you? You must under-stand that if you put portraits of me, naked, on display for all the people I know, I could no longer hold up my head in public."

She could hear the anger building in him. "This is art, Kathleen."

"This is me."

The CD ended, and the resulting silence empha-sized her words. She turned away from the paintings. "If you put me on display, I will be diminished. I will no longer be the woman you painted so magnifi-cently."

"But, Kathleen—"

She saw the argument coming, and she held up both hands to stop it. "These three paintings are works of genius, Foster. I understand your need to share them with the world, and I readily acknowledge that they could enhance your reputation a hundred-fold. Now... what do you want from me?"

"Your permission to show them."

"I can't give you my blessing. Not for an exhibit here in Denver, where too many people will delight in knowing more than they should about me."

This would have been so much easier if she could have called upon his love for her. But she was not yet sure that love existed. Yes, there was passion. But even their desire was unconsummated, unfulfilled. They still had only a sketchy outline of a relationship.

Kathleen knew her heart, knew she would never love another man as she loved Zachary Foster. But he was not privy to the year she'd spent in mourning and regret. A year that had made her stronger. Strong enough to hold her temper. Strong enough to walk away.

Slowly, she went past him to the door of his studio. "A limousine will pick you up at five o'clock. That's an hour from now."

"I have to show these paintings," he said.

Her hand rested on the doorknob. "It's your creative work, Foster. You own it. I showed you a glimpse of my naked soul, and you captured it on canvas. It's your decision."

She opened the door and stepped out into the brilliant sunlight of the late June afternoon.

As the heat touched her face, Kathleen comprehended the truth with a depth she had never known. *This* was the hard lesson she needed to learn, the answer to her fateful question about eternal love. She could not force Zachary Foster to return her feelings.

Couldn't demand that he love her. Couldn't buy his devotion.

There was only so much she could do. She had re-lived this day to discover that she could not control every facet of her life and fate. Zachary Foster would have to choose for himself.

Turning back to face him, she said, "There's nothing else I can say or do. I can't order you to obey me. Not even a princess can control the hearts of her subjects. It's up to you now, isn't it?"

"Yes," he said. There was something important in this moment. And Zach sensed it, like a change in the wind. The slight breeze through the open door brushed his face. And as Kathleen stood, completely motionless, backlit by the sun, he thought it might be the last time he would ever see her, that she was walking out of his life forever, leaving an enormous blank space. "Don't go, Kathleen."

"I'll be back. Five o'clock."

The door closed, leaving Zach in his studio with a sense of destiny, and a very big decision to make. Show the portraits and send his career skyrocketing. Or withhold these incredible paintings from public view? Show the paintings and lose Kathleen? Hide them and keep her?

A painful dilemma. If he'd been advising another artist, he would have told them to put the works on display and let the woman be damned. She'd known what she was doing when she posed, nearly naked. She could have refused, could have said no. It wasn't as if he'd forced her to strip. What the hell did she think he was painting when she exposed her breasts?

But she had wanted a Zachary Foster portrait for her own use, for herself. Because she had trusted him, she'd allowed him to take artistic liberties. Trust. How the hell could he betray her? How could he hurt her?

He ought to be grateful to her. She had given him a chance to indulge his vision. And the results were astounding.

The three paintings represented the finest work he'd done so far in his life. They surpassed anything he'd ever accomplished before. How could he keep from showing them?

He slipped another CD into the player. The dark, heavy, classical music by Wagner suited his mood. A rage was building within him. This wasn't fair. It wasn't right.

He'd fought his way up from abject poverty, from the streets. As an orphaned, illegitimate, destitute kid, his fate might well have been sealed. His one advantage had been his talent. Now he had a chance to make it big. And the dangerous, desirable heiress who'd inspired him was standing in his way.

Zach threw himself on the futon and stared at the paintings. Kathleen Welles knew nothing of his struggle. She couldn't imagine what it was like. She'd never suffered, had never known what it was to want something so badly you'd risk everything to get it.

He'd show the paintings. Damn, why should he care what she thought? He was nothing more to her than a rich girl's temporary diversion. He didn't kid himself about the possibility of a future between them. She might be willing to play around with him, might even make love with him. But they were utterly mismatched. The princess and the pauper. Ultimately, the society folks she feared would hold sway, and she'd dump him for a more suitable mate.

He took out his pocket watch. Less than an hour, and she'd be back with a limousine. A limo? That ought to show him how different they were. The princess could order up limousines with a snap of her beautiful fingers. And he had to fight to keep his window-design business going while he slaved at his art.

He turned over the watch in his hand and read his grandmother's initials. He could hear her voice in the back of his head, lecturing him about self-pity. There had been someone who believed in him. His grandma. She'd always told him that he could be something. What would she say he should do?

His fingers closed around the watch. Grandma knew what was right and what was wrong. She preached loyalty and truth. He knew what she would say. She'd tell him that it was wrong to betray the woman who had trusted him. Father Blaize would say the same. Given Kathleen's feelings, no matter how misguided they were, to show the paintings would be a violation. She'd be hurt.

Again, he looked at the paintings. They were so damned wonderful that he could hardly believe he'd had the skill to paint them. They were alive. Beautiful. Provocative. And profound. As long as they existed, he couldn't trust himself not to put them on display. There would always be the temptation.

Foster knew what he must do. He went to his work area and picked up an X-Acto blade. The razor-sharp edge glittered in the light.

He stood in front of the largest painting. The CD music crescendoed. He raised the knife.

Chapter Nine

At exactly ten minutes past four, Kathleen telephoned her mother's hospital room. Dr. Mathers was there.

"Is she all right?" Kathleen asked him.

"Yes. As you predicted, there was the onset of trauma. But we've been able to avert it. She's fine."

"Thank God! She didn't have a stroke?"

"She's fine," he repeated. "I'll be keeping her for about a week, testing her reaction to different medications."

"May I speak to her now?"

"Sure." He paused. "Kathleen, I want to apologize. I was abrupt with you, angry. Armitage was on target. It's hard for a doctor to acknowledge nonmedical forces that have an impact on life and death. The unexplained and the unexplainable."

"It's all right," she said.

"No, it's not. I set myself up as a tin god on a golf course, assuming that you knew nothing because you weren't qualified to know. I was wrong. Listen, Kathleen, I don't know how you got my name. I don't know what drove you to kidnap me. But I'm damned glad you did."

"I knew you were a good guy," she said. "And I'm the one who owes you a debt of thanks, Doctor. For saving my mother's life."

"I'll let you talk with her. Be brief. She needs rest."

Kathleen watched the minute hand on her watch as it ticked to four-fifteen.

In a tired voice, her mother said, "Hello, Kathleen."

"I'm so glad you're all right."

"The doctor tells me I'm going to have to change my life-style." She sighed. "He suggested a vacation. Can you imagine? I haven't taken a real vacation since your father and I went to Greece twelve years ago."

"Lucky for you," Kathleen said brightly, "that Welles already has a travel agent."

"He also told me I can't put in such long hours at the store. I can't take responsibility for everything. Can't work through lunch hour."

Kathleen smiled. "Sounds as if he's been talking to Helen."

"Yes, he has." Hannah was more spirited. "And she told him everything about my schedule, even my eating habits. I'm going to have to fire that woman. Either that, or give her a monumental raise."

"I vote for the pay increase," Kathleen said. "And a big promotion for me. While you're recovering, I'll be acting president at Welles."

"What? My darling, you're hardly able to show up at your office in time for lunch. How could you take on that much responsibility?"

"You'll be here to advise me, and Helen will keep me organized. You know as well as I do that this is what I ought to be doing with my life." For what she hoped was the last time in this waning twenty-four hours, she said, "Trust me."

"My dear Kathleen, I simply cannot—" The imperiousness faded from her mother's voice, and she actually giggled. "Oh, what the heck. You start on Monday."

"I will. Get some rest, Mother."

"I do feel awfully tired. As if I haven't slept in ten years. Not since your father... Oh, well, never mind all that."

Kathleen wanted to tell her about the time bubbles, that her father was still alive somewhere in time and memory. It would be such a comfort to Hannah. But Kathleen decided her mother had gone through enough for one day. "I love you, Mom."

Hannah sighed through the phone. "Good night, dear."

Kathleen hung up. At least this crisis had been handled successfully. Her mother was safe, under the care of a good doctor.

Her relationship with Zachary Foster was a different matter altogether. With only a half hour to prepare, Kathleen refused to rehash and second-guess. At his studio, she'd done what felt right. If he chose to show the paintings even as she was assuming greater responsibility and higher visibility at Welles, the embarrassment might be overwhelming. If ever there had been a time she needed to be respected, this was it.

But she had to trust him. It was his decision. Her future was in his strong, sensitive hands. Kathleen realized that that was a frightening thought, that trusting someone was almost harder than loving him.

If Foster cared more about his career than about her, he would show the paintings. And why *should* he care about her? Had she given him enough reason? She had no other hold on him, no leverage.

Clearly, the next seven hours were vital. She had to seduce him utterly, body and soul, prove her love to him and hope he loved her.

A few rapid phone calls confirmed her plans for the evening. Kathleen leapt into the shower, performed a high-speed beauty ritual and dressed in a flattering, batik silk, sarong-style dress. Though the swirling pattern of greens and blues shot through with silver fell to the floor, the sarong's slit was thigh-high. She selected a piece of jewelry shimmering with semiprecious gems of green and blue, then set it aside.

Foster knew the difference between precious and semiprecious. Between genuine and false. A year into the future he would tell her he wanted real diamonds for his display. And that was what she would wear tonight. A simple diamond necklace, bracelet and stud earrings.

Her condo intercom buzzed, and a woman's voice said, "Miss Welles? Your limo is here."

"Are you my driver?" Kathleen asked, suddenly unaccountably nervous.

"Yes, ma'am. My name is Artemis."

Artemis? Kathleen's fingers tightened on the receiver. Artemis was the Greek name for the Roman goddess, Diana. "Diana Marie? Is that you?"

"Excuse me, ma'am?"

"Nothing," Kathleen said. "I'll be right down."

As she descended from the tenth floor on the elevator, she considered. If the time merchant had turned up again, there had to be a reason. Did she bring a warning? Did she have more advice? In her appearance as Mrs. van Winkle, Diana Marie had offered Kathleen the chance to cancel the contract. Now, of course, that option was out of the question. Even if the situation with Foster worked out in the worst possible way, Kathleen had saved her mother a year of needless suffering. She would not trade that for anything.

Approaching the limo, she saw a robust blonde in a white uniform and visored hat. She was tall as an Amazon, as broad across the shoulders as a football player. Her features were masked by sunglasses.

"Diana Marie?"

"Artemis, ma'am."

But the voice held a familiar tone. "Let's not bother with the alias. I know who you are. What do you want?"

"We should be going. You don't want to be late."

When the driver efficiently held open the door, Kathleen thought for a moment that perhaps she'd made a mistake. But when she passed the tall woman, she impulsively snatched the sunglasses from her face. Dark, lively eyes stared back at her, eyes that had seen the wonders and tragedies of the ages.

"Why are you here?" Kathleen demanded.

"I don't much like being bested by a woman like you, Kathleen Welles. But I must admit, you've been very successful. Amazingly so. Most people who wish to buy or sell a day haven't made much impact on their lives or the lives of those around them. But you, you little upstart, have success within your grasp."

Kathleen didn't know how to respond to this back-handed compliment. Her instincts told her it would not be wise to offend this woman staring down at her from her superior height.

"Generally, the fates are not so kind," Artemis said. And with a wave of her arm, she transported them once more into formless space. Kathleen felt rather than saw the events of the coming year as they pertained to her mother. The modifications in life-style had transformed Hannah's health. Kathleen would still handle Welles, but it would not be because her mother was recovering from a debilitating stroke. It would be because her mother was learning to enjoy life.

Hannah would take up golf and give Dr. Mathers a run for his money. She would relax. She would attend the theater and go for long walks. Kathleen was left with a gentle, content impression of her mother sitting quietly on a mountaintop watching a red-and-gold sunset.

The vision faded, and they were in front of her condo once again. Kathleen felt reassured. She looked into the driver's dark eyes. "What about Foster? What's going to happen between us?"

"Will you find eternal love?" Her tone was caustic. "That remains to be seen."

"Thank you for showing me that my mother will be well."

"Don't thank me yet," said Diana Marie. "Your twenty-four hours have not ended. I've come to warn you, Kathleen, don't meddle beyond your own affairs. Some events will not change things for the best."

"What events? What are you talking about?"

Resuming the identity of a driver, she gestured to the open limo door. "Get in, Cinderella. Your pumpkin awaits."

Foster was waiting in the alley outside his studio. Though he still wore Levi's, he'd changed into a clean white shirt. He strode to the rear door. "Something came up. I can't go to dinner with you right now."

"But, Foster—"

"Sorry," he said simply. "I'll call you on your cellular phone when I'm done. We'll have our dinner later."

He ran to his van and fired up the engine, and in moments he was on his way out of the alley.

Kathleen turned on the limo's intercom. "Follow that van."

"I'd advise against it."

"You're my driver, aren't you? Do as I say."

The gears meshed, and the long white limo cruised out of the alley, tracking Foster's route.

On the north side of Colfax Avenue, he pulled over and parked. He ran from his van and jumped into the limo with Kathleen. "What the hell do you think you're doing?"

"Going for a drive."

"I don't want you in on this. Donny has a problem, and I've got to help him out."

Donny? The young man who worked at Foster's window-design company? "What's going on?"

"His younger brother is in trouble."

Immediately, Kathleen realized that if she accompanied Foster, she'd be guilty of the very meddling she had just been warned against. Still, she said, "Give me the address, and the limo will take us there."

"Not a chance."

She faced him, intensely aware of his strong, indomitable determination. He was a man with a purpose. His firm jaw was set as implacably as granite. His eyes were flint blue. But his stance did not intimidate her. These hours were hers. Theirs. "I've made plans for us."

"Stuff happens. Plans have to be changed."

"Have to be?" A twinge of temper tightened her muscles.

"This is important, Kathleen." His expression softened slightly as he met her gaze. "You've said this today, now it's my turn. Trust me."

"You don't understand, Foster. I've given you my trust." She could have destroyed those paintings. The last time she lived this day, that was exactly what she had done. "More trust than I've ever given anyone in my life."

"I need more."

"And when will it be enough?"

"When it's enough." His fingers balled into fists. "This is something I have to do. Donny needs my help, and I can't ignore the kid. That's not the way I run my life."

His life. A chilling insight dawned upon her. Though Kathleen recalled every minute of this day that had already occurred, she had no idea what Foster had been doing. A year ago or today. After she left his studio, she'd been at the hospital with her mother and had not seen him. What had he done during the remainder of the day? Had he been thrust into this problem with his assistant before? What had happened the first time?

The dilemma of changing the future struck her as it never had before. Though Kathleen had been certain of how she had wanted to alter her own, she didn't know the other events of Foster's day.

Suddenly, time was uncontrolled, uncertain, capricious. Though she'd carefully planned a spectacular evening, something in Foster's life was taking over.

Cocooned in the cool, silent limo interior, they were isolated from the outside world. And yet time was marching on, to Foster's tune as well as her own. What was she supposed to do? How could she avoid "meddling" in the life of the man she loved?

Kathleen pressed the intercom to speak with the driver. "Diana Marie?"

"My name is Artemis, ma'am."

"Artemis, do you know where I'm supposed to be going?"

"Only if you tell me, ma'am."

"Can't you help me?"

"Ma'am, I'm sure your destiny is in your hands."

She clicked the intercom off.

Foster was watching her. "What was that all about? More magic?"

"Could be. Are you going to give me the address?"

"If I don't, are you going to follow me?"

"Yes."

"Damn." He flicked on the intercom and gave an address, then turned back to Kathleen. "Satisfied?"

"Not yet."

"What do you want from me?"

"Everything," she said simply. "I want it all."

This should be their night. And if she didn't participate in his actions, the course of the future might be forever changed, and not in the ways she'd dreamed of. She sank back on the plush seat and closed her eyes. Time, she thought, was not a river plunging forward. Rather, it was a web sticky with complications that impeded progress from one strand to the next. How to creep forward, dragging the burden of the past, while driven pell-mell toward the future?

She understood, more deeply than ever before, that being in a relationship meant dealing with issues beyond her own, that other people's lives had the same depth and texture as her own. And that merging them was more complex than carbohydrates!

On her previous journey through these twenty-four hours, she had seen the nude portraits of herself as an impossible embarrassment, a cruel violation of her privacy. She had not considered Foster and his career as an artist. When she destroyed the pictures, slashing in her frenzied rage, his career had been affected in the year that followed. Had she destroyed his inspiration? Had she slashed through his dreams?

"I was so spoiled," she said. "I thought the whole world revolved around me."

"What the hell are you talking about?"

"You." She gazed at him. "Your life."

"Kathleen, have you been drinking?"

"No, thinking."

"Sometimes that's worse." At least he was smiling. Warming to her.

"About the portraits," she said.

"We don't have to talk about that." The warmth fled from his expression. "I've made my decision."

"Which is?"

"Mine," he said simply. "My decision."

"But it affects me. This is important to—"

To me, she'd meant to say. Me, me, me. Good grief, couldn't she think of anything but herself? Was she really so self-involved? So utterly selfish?

Wait. During the year she'd spent running Welles and making plans that affected a hundred employees, she'd developed some ability to empathize. Right now, right here, she had to use that experience. Kathleen swallowed hard. "It *is* your decision," she acknowledged. "And whatever you decide, I'll try to understand. But it's difficult, all this trusting."

He sat back in the seat, staring straight ahead.

She looked at him. "What happened to Donny's brother?"

"He ran away from home."

That didn't seem so terrible. Kathleen herself had run away from home many times, packing up her little lunch, taking along some Perrier.

"He's fifteen," Foster said.

Again, not dire. When Kathleen was sixteen and had an argument with her mother, she'd taken her Toyota, the first car she'd owned, to the mountains and stayed at their cabin for a whole day.

"He's taken a girl with him," Foster continued. "They have no money, and the girl's father is threatening to kill him."

"Kill a child?" Kathleen protested.

"According to Donny, the father has a vicious temper. He also has a gun." He glanced at her. "A real gun. That shoots real bullets. If Donny doesn't find the kids and make the father happy, somebody could end up real dead.''

This was the sort of story she read about in the newspaper. Shootings and street fights. Kathleen was definitely venturing out of her depth. And yet, this was the environment where Foster had lived, where he'd grown up. Didn't love mean that she accepted, and welcomed in, everything about him?

The limo parked in front of a row of dingy stucco apartments. Foster was instantly on the street. He sauntered up the cracked sidewalk toward a unit on the end where a screen door yawned.

Preparing to follow, Kathleen rested her hand on the door handle. Her diamond bracelet flashed against her delicately tanned wrist.

Through the intercom, her driver warned, "You weren't here the last time."

"No," Kathleen agreed.

"Don't get involved. There's nothing you can do."

But if she was going to be part of Foster's life, she needed to be part of everything. "Maybe I can help."

Kathleen let herself out of the car and slammed the heavy door. It wasn't in her nature to hide. She might have spent most of her life as a selfish, spoiled brat. But she wouldn't be a coward.

She joined Foster on the stoop. Through the screen door, she saw Donny and an older woman who sat on a threadbare sofa, sobbing loudly. As soon as Donny spied Foster, he came outside. His goofy attitude had been wiped away. His young face held an adult concern. "Can't let this happen. Chad's my brother. He's stupid, but he's still my kid brother."

Foster asked, "Do you know where they are?"

Donny shook his head. "Not in any of the usual places. They don't have much money, so they can't go far."

"And the girl's father? He's really dangerous?"

"Oh, yeah. He's a crazy man. Got a gun."

"I'll talk to him," Foster said. "He's got no reason to be mad at me. Maybe he has some idea where the kids are. Where's he live?"

"Around the corner, down a block. He's in a little house by the barbecue shack."

"What's his name?"

"Royce."

"Okay. You stay here with your mother. I'll be back."

He paid no attention to Kathleen. It was as if she didn't exist. And, in a way, maybe she didn't. After all, she hadn't been part of these events the first time they'd occurred.

She hurried along the sidewalk at his heels. Though she'd lived in Denver all her life, she had never ventured into this area. Where the lawns were dried earth, bereft of grass, and the paint peeled from the buildings. There were so many people, sitting on stoops, listening to loud music. So many songs. So many lives. And she had known nothing about them.

Foster slowed his pace, then stopped. "I'm taking you back to the limo. You don't belong here. The cost of your bracelet alone probably equals a year's wages for these people."

"But I belong with you."

"You'll be in the way. This isn't a game, Kathleen. This guy has a gun, and he's dangerous."

Which was exactly why she intended to tag along. How could she allow Foster to walk into danger alone? "I'll stay out of the way."

"I don't have time to argue with you," he muttered. "But when we get there, don't talk, okay?"

"Not a word."

She wasn't too worried. After all, he had obviously survived this encounter the last time. She'd seen him at work the very next day, and he hadn't been wounded.

Near the barbecue shack, the scent of sizzling meat and sauce permeated the air, making it feel hot and thick. Foster pushed open a creaking gate on a picket fence that looked as if it had been through a tornado. He tapped on the wood frame of a torn screen door. "Royce?" he called out. "I want to talk."

Kathleen watched a large, dark figure take shape behind the screen. The man was huge, bearlike.

"What d'ya want?" he growled.

"Are you Royce?"

"Who wants to know?"

"The name's Foster. Chad's older brother works for me."

"Yeah?" The big man wheezed when he spoke. "Seems to me this ain't none of your business."

"You're right. I don't even know Chad. That's why I can talk sense. I'm not in the middle of this."

"Chad." He turned his head and spat. "The kid took my daughter. He had no call to do that."

"Does she live here with you?"

"I'm taking care of her." He sounded defensive. "I buy her clothes and stuff. I feed the little bitch. When she gets back here I'm going to tan her hide, teach her a lesson. Why'd she go and do this to me?"

"Let me help you find her," Foster said.

The screen door popped open, and Royce came onto the porch. He was the scariest person Kathleen had ever seen. He was huge. His massive gut drooped over the waistband of his jeans. His shirt was filthy, sweat stained. His thinning black hair hung in greasy strands almost to his shoulders. His face was fat and mean. "Don't know where they went," he rumbled. "If I knew, I'd kill that little—"

"Does she have girlfriends? Somebody she hangs out with, might stay with?"

"Lots of friends. My little Angela is real popular. At least, she was before she started hanging out with Chad. My little angel. He messed her up. She says she's going to marry him."

"Is that so bad?"

"You don't get it." He shifted his belly and glared at Foster through tiny pig eyes. "She's my girl. I raised her, and there ain't nobody going to take her away from me."

Though Kathleen had never met Angela, she pitied the girl. What chance did she have in life? She lived in filth. Her father was a grotesque monster. How could anyone rise above these squalid circumstances?

Foster tried to get the names of her friends, but Royce didn't know anyone or wasn't telling. Over and over he repeated his intention to kill Chad. This was all Chad's fault. "He ruined her. Now he says he'll marry her. Forget it. Forget about it, Angela. You ain't fit to be married. You're mine," he snarled. "She's mine."

Foster turned to leave.

"Hey!" Royce shouted. "You find them. You bring her back here. Got it?"

Foster waved but said nothing. At the creaky gate, he spoke in a low voice to Kathleen. "I don't think there's much to worry about. He's too lazy to go looking."

"I didn't see a gun," she said.

"Back pocket of his jeans," Foster said. "But I think he's all threat and no action."

"Hey!" Royce yelled again. "You bring her back. You promise me you're going to bring my baby girl back here."

"You go to hell," Foster muttered.

There was the loud snap of a single pistol shot.

Chapter Ten

"Run!" Zach shouted.

Kathleen didn't need to be told twice. She hiked her long skirt up to her thighs and sprinted beside him. As they dodged along the street, Royce yelled after them.

There were screams, shouts, curses.

Kathleen flew around the corner, racing toward the limo.

Zach glanced back over his shoulder and saw Royce charging down the sidewalk like an enraged rhino.

Foot traffic on the street dispersed. Children ran inside. The people on the stoops took shelter. The air still throbbed with the heavy, thumping bass of the music. Cars still cruised on the street. But the sidewalks were deserted, empty.

The big man halted, wheezing like a bellows. Royce was in such wretched physical condition that the short run had exhausted him. He threw back his head, gulping for air. Then he shook his fist at the retreating forms of Zach and Kathleen. He yelled something unintelligible.

Zach couldn't make out the words, but he responded to the threat. And inside his head, there was a click, transforming him from a fairly civilized artist and the owner of a small business to a street-smart fighter.

He knew exactly what he must do. He had to face down Royce, beat him at his own savagery, or Donny's brother and his girlfriend would never draw a safe breath.

First, he made sure that Kathleen reached safety and was tucked away in the back of the limo. Then he rounded the corner and doubled back toward Royce, using parked cars for cover. A dark instinct directed his actions. He hated bullies.

Zach watched as the huge man turned away, stuck his gun into his back pocket and lumbered off, looking for him.

This was going to be easy, Zach thought. All he had to do was run down the street, tackle Royce and take his handgun. Once he was disarmed, the bully wouldn't be dangerous. Not if he was facing a grown man. Instead of a fifteen-year-old kid like Chad. Or his daughter, Angela.

Zach stepped out from behind cover. Adrenaline pumped through his veins. He prepared to charge.

"Foster!"

He heard the shout. Kathleen was running toward him.

He glanced toward Royce, who apparently hadn't heard her cry. From the rear, the man resembled a grizzly bear. Mean, pure mean. If he turned around, there was no way Zach could risk an approach. Royce didn't have to be strong or smart. He just had to aim and pull the trigger.

Kathleen reached his side.

"What the hell are you doing?" he demanded.

"Don't go after him."

He kept an eye on Royce. He'd halted in the middle of the sidewalk.

Zach dragged Kathleen roughly behind a car. "Stay here. Don't move."

"I won't let you go out there."

When he saw Royce reach for his gun, Zach ducked down behind the tail of a Ford. It was too late to surprise him.

Royce drew his handgun. There were angry yells from behind closed doors, but the big man swatted the air with one huge paw and yelled, "Shut up! All of you!"

Grumbling, he came toward them. He was within twenty feet of where they were crouched, hiding. They could hear his heavy breathing, his muttering. If only Royce would put the gun away, Zach thought. If only Kathleen hadn't tried to stop him.

Then Royce laughed, a disgusting, belching sound. "A limo. A goddamned limousine."

He turned around, his steps heavy, the gun in his hand, and proceeded down the sidewalk toward his house beside the barbecue shack.

Zach glared at Kathleen. "Why did you stop me?"

"I didn't want you to be hurt." Her voice caught in her throat. "That person is crazy."

Her cheeks were flushed. Her eyes sparkled. With fear? For him? If she'd been scared, she should have stayed out of trouble. "Are you okay?" he asked.

"Oh, sure, I'm just fine," she said sarcastically. "It's a real treat to have an enraged maniac shooting at me."

"You were the one who insisted on coming along."

"I'm glad I did."

"Oh, yeah. Me, too." He stood and watched as Royce reached the gate in his picket fence and shoved his way through. He climbed the two porch steps slowly and went back inside. "He's gone."

"Thank goodness."

"Listen to me, Kathleen. You don't belong here. You don't know what the hell is going on. Let me be the boss."

Stubbornly, she refused. "Not if you're going to endanger yourself."

"This wasn't dangerous." All he had planned to do was knock Royce on his fat butt, take his gun and leave. He wasn't looking for some kind of life-and-death struggle. He didn't have anything to prove, and he was much too smart to take crazy risks. He looked at her. "You wouldn't understand."

"Knock it off, Foster. Knock that chip off your shoulder."

"What chip?"

"The attitude that because you came from a less privileged background than mine, I can't possibly comprehend you."

"How could you?" An heiress like her could never really relate to a man like him. She wouldn't even want to. "Let's get back to your limo, okay?"

They walked slowly down the sidewalk. Around them, the street activities resumed.

"You know," Kathleen said, "I don't think you're being fair, Foster. I understand what's going on here."

"Do you?"

"Yes, indeed. That man shot at us. I'm conversant with the concept of survival." She took the cellular telephone from her purse.

"Don't bother calling the police," he advised. "It's our word against his. They can't arrest the guy if he claims he didn't do anything."

"I beg to differ. There were at least half a dozen witnesses. And I know a judge who will issue a search warrant for that dismal little house. Mr. Royce can quite easily be taken into custody, even if it's just for the night."

No doubt she was right. A woman like Kathleen Welles would number judges among her intimate friends. But Zachary Foster had spent too many years thinking of the police and the judicial system as adversaries. Back here in the old neighborhood, others would share that way of thinking.

"But I wasn't calling 911," Kathleen said archly.

"Who, then?"

"My caterer." She spoke into the telephone. "Hello, Jean-Pierre? We've been delayed." She paused. "Yes, I know the quiche must be served at a certain temperature." Again she paused, listening. "And the wine. Yes, yes, I know. You'll simply have to make do. I promise to telephone you at least ten minutes before we arrive."

Amazed, Zachary gaped at her. She'd been shot at, physically threatened on one of the meanest streets of Denver. That couldn't be an everyday occurrence for a princess. And yet, moments later, she was discussing the serving temperature of wine with a French chef. Calmly, she ended her phone call and turned to him. "What do we do next?"

He spoke slowly so that maybe, just possibly, she would listen to him. "This is very dangerous."

"I know."

"You could have been killed, Kathleen."

"But I wasn't. And neither were you. I suggest we avoid having that happen."

"Either you're the bravest woman I've ever known or you're crazier than Royce."

"I'm scared." She held out one slender hand, and he saw her fingers trembling like an aspen leaf in a high wind. "But I'm also in a hurry. I want this to be over."

"I never should have brought you here. No matter what you said. No matter—"

"But, in a way, I'm glad to be here," she said. "If I'm ever going to know you better, I need to understand what it's like to be in your world."

"That takes more than an afternoon." He stopped beside the limousine and leaned against the shiny front fender. "Visiting a prison is a whole lot different than being incarcerated."

"Coming here is a start," she said. "I know I can't live your life, Foster, but I want to know what influences formed you. The real you. Until now, you've had the advantage. You're acquainted with my lifestyle. For example, you could tell at a glance if my jewelry was diamonds or paste."

"It's real," he said.

"Just as I'm real," she stressed. "In spite of enjoying fine clothing, I'm not a plastic mannequin."

When he searched the depths of her incredible brown eyes, Zach indeed saw strength and intelligence, tolerance and tenderness. She *was* real, not just a giddy fairy-tale princess.

Abruptly, he said, "You're right, Kathleen. Let's get this mess taken care of."

"I'm so glad you see it my way. If we're much later for dinner, Jean-Pierre will throw a fit."

"There's a frightening thought," he said wryly. "Okay, let's check with Donny. I have an idea now where the kids might have gone."

They went back to the apartment where Donny's mother lived. She'd gone into the small bedroom, where she was trying to sleep. Quickly, Zach ex-

plained what had happened with Royce and advised
Donny to stay there to protect his mother in case
Royce built up enough energy to drag his gigantic body
around the corner. "Don't try to fight him," Zach
warned. "If you hear him coming, get out."

"I could take him," Donny said.

"Yeah," Zach agreed. "You could. But he's got a
gun."

"I can put my hands on an automatic."

"You shoot that pig and you'll go to jail," Zach
said. "He's not worth it. Promise me you won't go out
and get yourself a gun."

"I'm cool." He nodded. "But what do I do about
Chad? I gotta find him, man. He can't handle Royce.
He's a baby."

Not really, Zach thought. Babies didn't run off with
their girlfriends. They didn't propose marriage.
"You've checked with all his buddies?"

"Right away. No one knows a thing."

"Royce said Angela was talking marriage."

"Oh, hey. Whoa! You think they went to the
church?"

"Best place for them. I'll check it out. You stay
here," Zach repeated. "No guns. Take care of your
mother."

"Cool."

Zachary and Kathleen went back to the limo, and he
gave instructions to the driver.

In the mirror Kathleen saw the unspoken warning
in the driver's dark eyes. She knew she was "med-

dling.'' The moment she'd charged down the street to be at Foster's side, she'd taken a step toward changing a history she knew nothing about. But she couldn't avoid it, couldn't allow him to put himself into danger. If he'd been shot...

But, of course, he had not been hurt on the first time he lived this day. He'd survived. And so had Donny. Kathleen had seen them, healthy and well.

On the other hand, she'd never met Chad or Angela. They could have been hurt, even killed, by Royce. If saving their lives meant she would change the course of fate, Kathleen didn't know what to do. She simply couldn't *not* try to help.

As the limo started moving, Foster sprawled on the plush leather seat. ''I tell you, Kathleen, this is a great way to conduct a search. Chauffeur. Air-conditioning. The works. It gives me a little space to think.''

''About two fifteen-year-olds trying to get married? There really isn't too much to consider, is there? In the first place,'' she said, ''I don't think it's legal. In the second, I wonder why they'd want to. They have their whole lives in front of them.''

''Those lives probably look pretty awful. They're probably thinking that if they have each other, it will be easier.'' He shrugged. ''Or maybe she's pregnant.''

''Oh, no. I hadn't thought of that.''

''I hope not. That father of hers won't handle it well.''

''She can't go back to him,'' Kathleen said with a shudder. ''You heard what he said. He'll beat her.

Maybe even worse. I don't even want to think about it."

"If she's at the church, she'll find places she can go, people who can help her."

Their car glided to a soundless stop before a simple granite church with two square bell towers and a round, roseate stained-glass window over the entryway. It was the only place in this neighborhood where the limo might have looked appropriate. For a wedding. Or a funeral.

Foster opened Kathleen's door and took her arm as they climbed the stairs. "Must be a lucky church. Both of my brothers got married here," he said. "And they both found good women and stayed married."

"And you? Why didn't you ever take that long walk down a short aisle?" Kathleen probed.

"Never found the right woman."

Could that be about to change? Kathleen wondered, hoped.

As they entered the cool nave with its high vaulted ceiling, a surreal feeling washed through Zach. He remembered his brothers' weddings, when he'd been best man, in a tuxedo with a rose in his lapel. Organ music, the wedding march, haunted the corners of his mind.

As if in the periphery of his vision, he noticed movement. A bride. Kathleen! She was dressed in the purest white, but her bouquet was a riot of red and blue and purple blossoms. A lacy bodice outlined her breasts. A veil covered her face, but the sheer material did not hide the lively flash of her eyes or the impish grin that turned up the corners of her mouth.

He turned his head and looked directly at her, erasing the vision his imagination had produced. She wore a sarong, in blue and green, but the grin was there.

"What about you?" he asked. "Why aren't you married to some lawyer or doctor?"

"Because I'm not in love with a lawyer or a doctor."

The church was empty except for two nuns in old-fashioned habits kneeling at the rail near the altar. Zach directed Kathleen to an exit near the front. "Let's go next door to the rectory."

They passed through a small garden, where a statue of Mary presided over a bed of roses. At the rectory, they climbed five steps to a wide porch and knocked at the door.

A white-haired priest wearing a black suit and stiff white collar answered. In a deep, melodious voice, he said, "Zachary Foster! It's good to see you, son."

"Same here." The two men shook hands warmly. "Father Blaize, this is Kathleen Welles."

"It's about time," he said. "I thought this young man would never get married."

Kathleen sputtered as she shook his hand. "That's not, I mean, we're not—"

"We're not here to get married," Zach said.

"Pity! She's a beautiful young woman, Zachary."

Father Blaize stepped out onto the porch to join his visitors, explaining that it was very hot indoors. He was ever looking out for the best interests of his flock—including a black sheep like himself, Zach thought.

He had the utmost respect for this old priest, and he owed him a debt of gratitude. Father Blaize had always encouraged his artwork. In the early years, he had even commissioned a portrait for the church, paying a grand sum that happened to exactly match the amount Zach needed for art-school tuition.

"Haven't we met?" he asked Kathleen.

"I don't believe we have," she calculated. But she'd recognized him, too. During the coming year, when she'd be acting president at Welles, she and Father Blaize would share a dais at a fund-raising banquet for Mercy Hospital.

"Very strange." He raised his bushy eyebrows. "I seem to be wanting to ask after your mother."

"She's much better." Kathleen had said these very words before. "But I would appreciate your prayers for her."

"Done." He transferred his twinkling gaze to Zach. "What can I do for you, son?"

"I'm looking for Chad and Angela."

"And why might that be?"

Kathleen noticed that Father Blaize did not deny that the two young people were there.

"Chad's brother, Donny, works for me," Foster said. "He told me the kids were in trouble. I went to talk to Angela's father, almost got shot in the back, and decided Royce was serious about killing Chad for stealing his daughter."

"Royce doesn't own Angela," Kathleen added.

"Unfortunately," said Father Blaize, "he's her father, and that does give him a legal hold."

The priest raised his gaze skyward, perhaps looking for guidance, and a slight breeze ruffled the white hair above his collar. Still, he admitted nothing.

Finally Zach said, "You have them here, don't you?"

"They're not here at the rectory."

"But you know where they are."

"Chad and Angela are in a safe place. They asked me to marry them. Can't do that, of course. But they do seem to be in love."

"At fifteen?" Kathleen couldn't help questioning.

"Juliet was younger," Father Blaize reminded her. "I think Romeo was all of sixteen."

"Right," Zach said. "Great comparison, Father. That story didn't exactly have a happy ending. If I remember right, everybody was dead in the last act. I think we can come up with a better alternative for Chad and Angela."

"Rest assured that we will be talking with social services and shelters. The young woman cannot be returned to her natural father's home. If you like, you might inform Donny and his mother that the young people are fine." He paused. "You might also tell Donny that it's been quite some time since his last confession."

Zach chuckled. "I'll bet Donny's confessions are pretty interesting material."

"Hush, Zachary. You're speaking of a sacrament."

Suddenly, there was a ruckus behind them. Royce lumbered through the garden, past the delicate marble Mary. His face red with the effort of propelling his huge bulk forward, he might have been laughable—except for the gun.

"Think you're smart?" he yelled. "You think you're so damn smart in your big fancy limo? Made it easy to follow you. Easy!"

He raised his pistol, aimed at them. "Okay, Father. Where's my Angela?"

In Kathleen's mind, everything froze, stood completely still. She tried to make sense of this timeless moment. In the way it had happened before, neither Foster nor Father Blaize had been killed. She'd seen them both during the coming year. They had survived.

But she had altered the past. Royce had found them because of the limousine, the limo she'd hired today. Her gaze darted between the two men who stood on either side of her. If one of them was killed because of her meddling, she could not bear it.

She saw Royce take another step forward. Every tick of the clock dragged like an hour, giving her an eternity of second-guesses. What had she done? She hadn't meant for anything to go so terribly wrong. How would the future be altered because of this past?

Less than fifteen feet away, Royce couldn't miss.

"Where is she?" he roared. "I want my daughter back!"

Only ten feet away. Kathleen sensed the pressure of his finger upon the trigger. He would shoot. He would shoot to kill.

"No!" she screamed.

A shot rang out.

And Royce spun around. He doubled over in pain, clutching the hand that had held the pistol.

From behind him and to the left, she saw Diana Marie in her guise as Artemis, the chauffeur. She held a long-barreled revolver, a weapon that looked as if it had come straight out of the Old West.

Zach was already down the stairs. He picked Royce's gun out of the rosebushes and nodded toward Artemis. "That was one hell of a shot, lady."

"I drive diplomats. I know how to do bodyguard work."

Kathleen was on the phone, calling the police. After the first call for assistance went through, she handed the cellular unit to Father Blaize and went toward Diana Marie.

Looking up into the woman's dark eyes, she said, "Thank you."

"You'd tampered with things to save that man of yours. I couldn't let the future be destroyed."

"What would have happened?"

"Father Blaize would have been killed. He's an old man, but he still has some important work left to do."

"Thank you," Kathleen said again, from her heart. "After this, it's up to you."

Kathleen smiled. "I'll miss you, Time Merchant."

Artemis turned away, mumbling something under her breath. It sounded to Kathleen as if she were wishing her good luck.

Chapter Eleven

Earlier that day, Kathleen and Foster had spoken of clouds with silver linings. Now she decided that the description suited his old neighborhood. When the darkness of Royce and his storm of evil had passed, the silver revealed itself. The radiance was beautiful, Kathleen thought. Caring people, good people, appeared from nowhere to console the endangered threesome and offer iced tea. Kathleen sat on a stone bench in the rectory garden, overwhelmed by their kindness.

She imagined that Foster's beloved grandmother had been like these folks. Struggling with poverty but not beaten by it. And glad to unselfishly offer what comfort she could.

The police arrived quickly, and, due to the influence of Father Blaize, Royce was taken into custody with few questions asked of Artemis. Which was fortunate, Kathleen thought, because she wasn't sure how Diana Marie managed these identity changes. Did she have proper credentials as she flitted across the days and years as easily as other people crossed the street?

As Kathleen watched the outpouring of concern for Father Blaize and the crew of old buddies who encircled Foster, she wondered how this situation had worked out the first time around. To be sure, she had meddled. If she hadn't raced back to stop Foster from taking on Royce, the big man wouldn't have seen the limo and come after them with his gun. But if he hadn't been arrested, would he have gotten his hands on Angela and Chad?

Since Diana Marie had engineered the outcome, Kathleen assumed that destiny had not been significantly altered. Her meddling had not torn the fabric of time asunder. But she would never know how helpful or how harmful her actions had been in influencing these moments.

When Father Blaize came and sat beside her, she asked, "What's going to happen to Chad and Angela?"

"The last act won't be *Romeo and Juliet*. That I can promise."

"She won't have to go back to that awful father of hers, will she?"

"There are facilities available for abused young people. Not nearly as many as are needed, but we will find a way. And I will be recommending counseling for everyone."

He tilted his head to catch the waning rays of the sunset on his face. He looked positively saintly, unconsciously creating a magnificent portrait of light and shadow. Kathleen noticed that Foster, still standing in the midst of his friends, was observing them. "That's my usual formula," Father Blaize said. "Counseling, common sense and prayer."

"I like your approach, Father. But we can't leave everything to the Lord, can we?" She unfastened the clasp on her diamond bracelet and placed the jewelry in his hand. "I want to help."

"Bless you, Kathleen."

"Pray for me, too." She glanced over toward Foster, who was now talking earnestly with Donny. "I might need a small miracle."

"No guarantees," he said.

She looked up sharply. Those were the words Diana Marie had used. Was it possible that she and the father were a team, that they had engineered this whole day? Kathleen shook her head in denial. To even consider such an unlikely duo, she must be overly tired. Every minute of this day had been packed, and the stress was taking a toll on her energy. How tired, then, must Foster be?

She watched him talking and laughing. She saw a hint of exhaustion in the way he rubbed his eyes and wearily pushed his hair off his forehead. He stretched and yawned as he said his goodbyes. It would be the height of irony if she were defeated, in these waning hours of her day, by something as simple as lack of sleep.

When they finally climbed back into the limo, he leaned his head against the seat and closed his eyes, his long legs stretched out in front of him.

"No rest for the wicked," she teased.

"What a day!"

Her own tiredness hung over her like a threatening cloud, but Kathleen had the surging awareness that today was her last and only chance to make Zachary Foster fall in love with her.

Ironically, the most important weapon in her arsenal of seduction might be caffeine. She checked the time on her wristwatch. It was almost seven o'clock. Only five hours left in her day!

Leaning across the seat, she lightly brushed his lips with her own. "Please don't fall asleep, Foster. Please."

Without opening his eyes, he said, "Do you remember Salvador Dalí, the surrealist?"

"The artist who painted the melting clocks," she said. She had never understood that picture. Until today.

"Dalí hated to waste time with sleep. He would only consent to rest while sitting upright in a chair, holding a heavy spoon in his hand. When he was near enough to sleep to drop the spoon, the sound of it clattering to the floor would wake him up."

"Have you ever done that?"

"Hell, no. I love sleep."

She studied his features in repose. High cheekbones sharply outlined the upper portion of his face.

A strong jaw protruded stubbornly, even when he relaxed. A sense of possessiveness came over her, as if she owned that handsome face, as if he would be her own to hold and admire for all eternity.

It had to be so! Kathleen could not live with another alternative. She was helplessly, hopelessly in love with him. And now she must convince him that he loved her, too.

Before they reached their destination, she made one last call to inform the waiting chef that they were on their way. She repaired her makeup, brushed her hair. When they arrived, she lightly tapped Foster's shoulder. "We're here."

"Okay, right." He squinted hard as he opened his eyes. "Here?" He stared through the window. "Kathleen, this is the Denver Art Museum."

"Tonight, it's ours."

"You're amazing! How did you manage to—"

"Simple. I've done a lot of volunteer work and fund-raising. I know which strings to pull."

"But the art museum?" He still couldn't believe it.

When the chauffeur held the door for them, Kathleen impulsively hugged the big blonde.

The physical contrast between the two females caused Zach to smile. Kathleen was lithe and dark. The driver was Rubenesque. And Zach wondered. There was something familiar about that driver, but he couldn't place her.

He shrugged off his thoughts. Throughout the day, he'd had an uneasy sense of déjà vu, as if he'd been down this road before.

He held out his arm to escort Kathleen into their remarkable dining room. The glass-brick building stood seven stories high with a unique parapet that drew the gaze upward toward the magnificent Rocky Mountains.

Less than two years ago, at the opening for a show of local talent, Zach hadn't been able to get his foot in the door. Now he was marching inside after-hours, as if he owned the place.

"I could get accustomed to being rich," he said.

"Could you?"

Her tone was serious. Surprisingly so. He glanced down at her. She looked on edge. Beneath her makeup, a shadow of exhaustion bruised the delicate skin below her eyes. Her cheeks were drawn and tired, yet her rich brown eyes sizzled with unquenchable, mesmerizing energy.

"Could you, Foster?" she repeated.

"I forgot the question," he admitted.

"We'll talk about it later," she promised as they strolled up to the cylindrical entryway.

A uniformed guard unlocked the doors and ushered them inside. "You're to take the elevator directly to the fifth floor, Miss Welles," he said. "No stopping in between."

"Thank you." Zachary guided her to the bank of elevators. "The fifth floor. Impressionists. They taught us new ways to capture color and emotion."

"Like your paintings of me," she said quietly.

When the elevator doors opened, Kathleen stepped out before him, smiled and gestured. Like magic, there was music, a jazz quartet playing "Summertime." She guided him into a room with oddly shaped windows offering glimpses of the mountains. In the center of the room, on an Oriental carpet, an elegant dining table had been set with a white linen tablecloth, heavy silverware, delicate crystal and a bouquet of purple roses.

The eating arrangements were beautiful, and on the walls was a feast for the eyes.

"Do you like it?" she whispered. She'd hoped the fine art would heighten his senses, engage his emotions, and that finally he would see her with different eyes. "Foster, do you like it?"

"I love it." He caught Kathleen's hand and squeezed her fingers. He was so touched that his voice was husky with emotion.

"I love it," he repeated. He looked around at the paintings that, for a few hours, would be theirs alone. "I feel like I've died and gone to heaven."

A chef in a high hat and white jacket stepped toward them. He ushered Kathleen to her seat but directed his comments toward Foster. "You are most fortunate," he said in a thick French accent. "Because I know Mademoiselle Kathleen so very well, I expected her to be late. I have prepared a menu that has not spoiled with tardiness."

"Thank you, Jean-Pierre." She introduced him to Foster.

"I am honored," Jean-Pierre said. "I know your work."

"You do? How?" Since Zach didn't travel among the circle of people who actually purchased his paintings, he didn't often bump into people who knew him as an artist.

Jean-Pierre continued, "I have catered in homes where your portraits are on display. Magnificent."

The Frenchman described four paintings in such glowing detail that Zach felt uncomfortable. He murmured his thanks.

"And now," Jean-Pierre announced, "we begin. Monsieur Foster, this is my art. Cuisine. I hope it will be worthy of your palate."

He uncorked a bottle of French wine, offered it for approval and, like the experienced server he was, retreated to allow them privacy.

Foster leaned back in his chair and gazed fondly at the woman who had managed to arrange such an amazing treat—all in the midst of saving her mother's life and joining him in the rescue of Chad and Angela. "Is there anything you can't do?"

"I'm a buyer," she said.

"That's your job, but this—"

"Actually," she interrupted, "buying is my skill. I've learned to recognize quality, and I'm able to negotiate to get it. But I'm not good at creating on my own. Not like you."

"But this..." He gestured around the room, allowing his gaze to consume the rich pastel glow of a small Degas. "This is inspired, Kathleen."

She blessed him with a delicate smile, and her expression eclipsed the exhaustion that crept at the edges of his consciousness. She was like the sun, permeating life with elegant brightness. No, he thought, the moon. Mysterious and lovely. Her black hair shimmered, and her diamond earrings twinkled like starlight. Her eyes held a promise of sweet sensuality. Definitely a princess of the moon.

Surrounded by art, Zach couldn't take his eyes off the woman opposite him. A diamond necklace rested in the hollow at the base of her throat, emphasizing her delicate collarbone and the smooth span of her bared shoulders. He could just glimpse the dark crevice between her breasts as she lifted her wineglass to her lips. Her fingers and wrist were perfection. Suddenly, he noticed something. "Weren't you wearing a bracelet?"

"I...took it off."

Her voice was breathy, sexy as hell, and it had Zach thinking of taking other things off.

Suddenly, she asked, "*Could* you become accustomed to this, Foster?"

"Your world is a beautiful place," he admitted. "Like paradise. But it doesn't feel like home to me."

"Not like your old neighborhood?"

He shook his head. "Don't romanticize that, Kathleen. I don't. There's nothing noble or brave about being broke. It happens. You live with it. If you're smart enough and lucky enough, you get out of it. When I go back, it's because of the people. Guys like Donny. And Father Blaize."

"He's an extraordinary man."

"Yeah, he is. There's a lot of good people where I grew up. But the neighborhood? That's not my home."

Jean-Pierre reappeared with a serving cart containing a crusty loaf of warmed bread, sweet butter and a silver tureen of chilled soup. "Vichyssoise," he announced as he ladled their servings into china bowls, then vanished again.

The sight and smell of food reminded Zach that he had barely eaten all day.

"Everywhere is my home," he said after sampling the wonderful soup. "And nowhere."

"If I had to pick a single place to call home, I guess it would be the store," Kathleen said. She tasted the wine, a delicious contrast with the heavy soup. "I guess that sounds a little silly, having a store for a home. But being at Welles makes me feel grounded."

"What happens if your mother ever decides to sell?"

"Sell? Mother? No way, Foster. During the past couple of years, we have been in the red. But I have some ideas on how to turn that around."

"So you're becoming quite a businesswoman."

"I guess so."

Kathleen was not entirely pleased with this turn in the conversation. She wanted to be seductive, to drive him wild with desire. And she was playing for keeps. It made her nervous.

As if sensing her distress, Foster reached across the table and took her hand in his. She felt a tremor of delight at the physical contact.

"A businesswoman. A buyer. And also a beauty," he said. "The most fascinating woman I've ever known."

She should have had a follow-up, a bit of sexy repartee. But she was tongue-tied, gazing helplessly into the most wonderful blue eyes in the world. His eyes. She wished she could climb inside his head and force him to see her the way she wanted him to: as his life partner, as the woman he would live with for all eternity.

But she'd have to lead him so carefully that he had no idea he was being led. She pushed back her chair. "Let's take a look around. This is the first time I've been here without a crowd to get between me and the art."

Wineglasses in hand, they toured the room slowly, appreciating the delicacy of brushwork and subtle shadings of color. More than once, Kathleen was tempted to compare the masterpieces displayed in the museum with the portraits Foster had done of her. But that topic was best left untouched.

After they made love, and he *felt* how much she loved him, she would ask him again not to display the pictures. Then he would not refuse. Would he?

Purposefully, she brushed up against him. She rested her hand on his shoulder and leaned against his body, allowing him to feel the swell of her breast. They were viewing one of Monet's water lilies, drinking in the hypnotic nuances of color and light. When she gazed up into Foster's eyes and he looked back at her, she saw the brilliance of Monet reflected there. He leaned closer, their lips met, and the moment was so perfect it took her breath away.

"I think I'm getting a little tipsy," she said.

He laughed. "This is pretty damned heady, you know. Not to mention decadent. Drinking wine in an exclusive museum."

She giggled. "But can't you just imagine these artists, these French Impressionists, swigging their wine and tearing off chunks of bread in an outdoor café on the Left Bank in Paris?"

He nodded. "That whole lost-generation thing."

"Living in the moment."

And the moments were passing quickly. Soon, too soon, this enchanted day would be over.

Jean-Pierre came to serve them a succulent crab quiche with a perfect, flaky crust, and he hovered nearby until they'd returned to the table and taken their first bites.

Kathleen groaned with sheer pleasure. "Jean-Pierre, you've outdone yourself."

He bobbed his head and aimed his attention at Foster. "Monsieur?"

"It's damned good. You deserve a medal, Jean-Pierre."

"I am touched." When the chef stepped back, his eyes were moist with tears. "I shall cook for you again, Monsieur Foster. But we shall have better timing." He gave a happy nod and retreated.

Under her breath, Kathleen said, "I guess I'm not known for my punctuality."

"But you're worth the wait," he said gallantly. "Besides, better later than never."

Never? The word echoed in her mind. It was now or never, she remembered. Her time was almost gone. A frantic urgency compelled her. And yet, this ultimate evening of seduction must be careful, planned . . . and permanent.

In the periphery of her vision, at the edge of time, she glimpsed another museum. She knew it was in another time. A bubble of time, once again appearing unbidden. Kathleen saw a long hallway with paintings carefully lit and displayed.

Then she saw herself, as an old woman with a long white braid. She stood before a portrait. The full-length nude that Foster had painted. With her ancient hand, she reached toward the canvas, trying to grasp the light. The memory.

The tears rose up in her eyes as she gazed across the table at him and felt the ache of separation. Because she knew that the vision she'd had was of the future. And she had been alone.

Chapter Twelve

Returning to the here and now, Kathleen swallowed the lump of fear that had lodged in her throat. The sense of regret that she'd lived with for one year threatened to overcome her, to ruin the rest of this day when she needed the slate to be clean and fresh. She struggled to regain her composure. But the vision had been so real. She'd felt as if she could reach out and touch her aged self. And the portrait! It was a beautiful vessel containing her youth. How had she ever destroyed such a masterpiece?

On the other hand, could she allow it to survive? If she really had glimpsed the future, the portrait was on display. In a museum. For everyone to see.

"Kathleen?"

Though she averted her gaze, she could feel Foster's scrutiny. She was behaving all wrong. She needed to be seductive and lighthearted... Instead...

"Kathleen, what's wrong? You look like you're about to cry."

"From happiness?" She forced her lips to smile.

"Not a chance. I can see the sadness here." He touched the corner of her mouth. "And here." He lightly stroked her temple. "It's the secret you've been keeping all day. Tell me, Kathleen."

How could she? If she began to tell him about the first time she'd lived this day, she would reveal herself as a monster who had slashed his finest work. She would remind him of the year when he had despised the sight of her. No, it was better to keep her secret. "It's okay. Let's enjoy Jean-Pierre's quiche first."

They dined in silence. In her mind, she could hear the minutes ticking away. It was almost eight o'clock. Only four hours left.

The chef reappeared with large plates containing steamed lobster, melted butter and asparagus tips in a light sauce.

Foster offered Jean-Pierre a catalog of praise that would have made a less egotistical chef blush.

If Kathleen could have fought back her sense of panic, she would have been delighted. Everything else was going so beautifully. The music. The food. The surroundings. It was all perfect. Except for her. She couldn't play her own part in this all-important seduction. She tried to infuse her voice with appropriate enthusiasm. "Jean-Pierre, how did you manage lobster? I know you're using limited cooking facilities in the employee lounge."

"I adapt." He placed a plate in front of her and snapped his fingers. "Many times, I have prepared gourmet meals on camping trips over an open fire. I need only boiling water." He set the second plate before Zach. "And voilà!" He opened another bottle of wine and poured. "Lobster is simple."

Foster asked, "You think I could do it?"

"A brilliant artist such as yourself? But of course. As you know, men are the best chefs."

"Don't be absurd," Kathleen said. "Fine cooking has nothing to do with gender."

The Frenchman's shrug was eloquent. "Between men and women, there are always differences."

"Vive la différence," Foster said wryly. "Tell me, Jean-Pierre, what do you think of a woman who keeps secrets?"

"She is the only sort of lady worth knowing. A woman of mystery." He gave a sly smile. "To reveal too much is an error."

"But how can you trust her?"

"Trust a lady? Oh, *monsieur,* you make a joke?"

Kathleen could have lectured him on the trustworthiness of her sex, but she preferred to make a point with Foster. "You see? Jean-Pierre understands how important it is for women to retain an aura of mystery."

"Does he?" Foster tasted the wine and again found it magnificent. "Are you married, Jean-Pierre?"

"I am a gourmet. I enjoy many tastes. To stay with only one woman? It would be to confine myself to one spice. To cook only beef."

He bowed from the waist and left them alone.

It was Foster's turn to gloat. "You see?"

"What?"

"When you're busy taking a sample of everything in a skirt, a woman's mystery is important. But when it's a meaningful relationship, trust and honesty are important."

Her hopes lifted. He seemed to be talking about commitment. "What are you saying, Foster?"

"Pointing out the obvious, princess."

She wanted to probe deeper. There wasn't enough time to be subtle. But she couldn't very well come right out and ask if he was calling *their* relationship meaningful.

She attacked her lobster, dipping the meat from the tail in drawn butter. "Well, I'm keeping my secrets," she declared. "I think I prefer to remain a woman of mystery."

Foster licked his lips, savoring the meal. "But I want to know what makes you smile and what makes you cry. I want to touch that wild part inside you that I keep catching glimpses of."

"But if you knew everything about me, I'd be boring as an old shoe."

"I could never know everything, Kathleen. Even if I did, you're changing every day, every minute." He took out his silver pocket watch. "It's eight-fifteen. We've been here for little more than an hour, and you've surprised me at least half a dozen times."

"Does that bother you?"

"The truth?" He gazed across their private dining table and deep into her eyes. "You excite the hell out of me."

This was exactly what she had hoped for! Exactly what she wanted! She lowered her lashes and gave him a slow, seductive look, thinking of how wonderful it would be when she finally felt his body against hers, of the intense fulfillment she would feel. Finally, she felt like a temptress, a seductress. "How excited are you, Foster?"

"I think you know."

"Tell me."

"I want to make love to you," he said. "Tonight."

Her heart soared into the stratosphere. It wasn't a marriage proposal. It wasn't even a statement of love or commitment. But it sealed her fate for the evening. Perhaps it would seal her destiny.

They finished the meal with a simple flan and strawberries, complimented Jean-Pierre lavishly, listened to one more smooth jazz number from the quartet and left.

Outside, night had settled on the city. The wine and anticipation generated a powerful heat within her, and Kathleen was grateful for the caress of a cool evening breeze across her cheeks. She instructed Artemis to drop them off at her condominium.

The woman's eyes widened with concern, but Kathleen didn't care. This was her fate! Love eternal! She was going to make love to Foster for the final hours of this most wonderful day.

When she snuggled up next to him in the back of the limo, her guard was down and she spoke from the heart. "This is all I've dreamed of for a year. For a whole long miserable year, I've wished and yearned. And I'm so happy."

"For a year?"

"Seems like a year," she corrected.

"You know, Kathleen, that's the first thing you said to me last night. When you showed up on my doorstep with your new haircut."

"Does it matter?" she asked, lightly kissing his cheek.

"Tell me what's going on, princess. Tell me why today is so different from all the days that have come before."

"Magic," she whispered in his ear, and she nibbled lightly on the lobe. "Enchantment." Did she dare say love?

"Watch it, princess." A shudder raked across his shoulders. He could feel himself becoming aroused. "Or I might attack you right here."

"Then I'll wait," she teased, scooting away from him, heightening the anticipation. "The moment must be perfect."

"You don't have something special planned, do you?" She'd pulled off some pretty spectacular feats this evening, and he wasn't sure what else she had in mind. "I mean, we're not going to get to your place and find Dr. Ruth called in as a consultant, are we?"

"I think we can figure out the moves all by ourselves," she said.

"I'll start here." His fingers traced her lips, and her tongue crept out to tease him.

His hand rested on her bare knee. "You won't get away from me tonight, Kathleen."

"I don't want to." She rested her hand on his as his fingers eased up her thigh. "I wish we had more time."

"We have the rest of our lives."

"Not really. We don't own time. It's borrowed. From day to day. From midnight to midnight."

Zach sensed that she was talking about something completely different. Her magic again? "Is something going to happen at midnight? You've talked about midnight before."

"What could happen?"

But he sensed her hesitation. A shifting from wanton desire to a more guarded posture.

"Is that it, Kathleen? What's going to happen at midnight?"

"I don't know. I can't read the future."

He removed his hand from her leg and leaned back against the seat. Though his belly was full, the wine had left a pleasant buzz and he had a beautiful woman in his arms, Zach was not content. In the center of his desire was a question. A disharmony. He had to figure it out.

"Last night you came to me a little after midnight. And you were different than before. More centered and a hell of a lot more desirable. We spent half the

day chasing down a doctor because you knew your
mother would have a stroke at exactly four-fifteen.
Then there's all this business with a fortune-teller and
Mrs. van Winkle."

"So?"

"Am I being jerked around like some stupid male
fish who went for the lure and got snagged?"

"I hope I've caught you." Her soft brown eyes
searched his face. "Foster, let it all go. Relax. Think
of the moment."

"I don't want anything standing between us."

The limo stopped. They had arrived at her building. "I will tell you," she said. "Before midnight."

Only two and a half hours. He could wait. "Is that
a guarantee?"

"There are no guarantees in life." There was a catch
in her voice.

Artemis opened the limo door. Finally, Kathleen
understood why Diana Marie, and even Father Blaize,
had been so hesitant. Kathleen could not engineer her
destiny. There were no guarantees. There was only
emotion. That was the magic. Love was the magic,
and no one could guarantee love.

Kathleen shook the driver's hand. "Thank you,
Diana Marie, for giving me this chance."

"Goodbye, Kathleen. Until we meet again."

"Will we meet again?"

"Actually, I rather hope not. Our association, my
dear, has been most time-consuming."

Kathleen glanced up toward her tenth-floor condominium. "I don't suppose you can tell me what happens next."

"It's up to you. And to him." She added, "You must not forget. He has his own life, his own future. You might be able to direct other people, but you cannot control them."

"I guess not."

"Kathleen?" She held out the palm of her hand. "I expect an excellent tip for my services this evening."

Kathleen emptied her wallet into the driver's hand.

Then she joined Foster on the sidewalk and led the way into her foyer and into the elevator. She spoke not a word. Nor did he. The future was now.

When the elevator stopped on her floor, he took out his watch and checked the time. "It's two hours and twenty-five minutes until midnight."

"Then I turn into a pumpkin," she said, unlocking her door. "If I gave you a glass slipper, would you bother to search for me?"

"I'm not Prince Charming."

"And I'm not Cinderella, either." She showed him inside and turned on the light. "I always thought she was a little annoying. Sitting around in the ashes and whining until a fairy godmother came and solved all her problems."

"How would you have done the fairy tale differently?"

In familiar surroundings, Kathleen felt her spirit returning. "How would I have done it? Well, first off,

I wouldn't have accepted the whole scullery-maid routine. I would have hired an attorney and sued my wicked stepmother for harassment."

"Very efficient," he said.

She faced him, hands on hips. "And I wouldn't have played games with the prince. I would look him straight in the eye." She looked Foster in the eye. "And I would have said . . ." She moved close to him. "I find you very attractive. I'd like to spend my happily ever after with you."

"Is that what you would say?"

Kathleen had no more time for plans or artifice. "I want to make love to you."

They stood close but not touching. The stillness of the night wrapped around them. Every sound was amplified. Her whisper echoed. "I want you to make love to me."

He caught hold of her waist, pulled her close. The cooled air of her condominium was not enough to douse the wildfire that raged within her. She was burning with a magnificent heat. Her light sarong felt hot against her skin.

His kiss sent the flames licking higher, until she felt she would be consumed by passion. When his tongue tasted the slick interior of her mouth, Kathleen responded voraciously. Her desire for him raged within her.

His need equaled her own. She could feel it in the imprint of his hand on her back. She could taste it in his mouth. She could hardly bear to wait another moment. Yet she reveled in the heat, the passion, the promise of earth-shaking ecstasy that soon would be theirs.

Separating herself from him, breathing hard, she said, "This way."

In her bedroom, she left the lights off, turned down the quilt and took him to the sliding-glass door that led onto a balcony. The twinkling lights of Denver lay beneath them like a kingdom. Overhead the stars shed soft light upon them.

"So many nights, I've stood out here alone."

"Not anymore, Kathleen."

She pointed across the treetops. "Over there is Welles. You can't actually see the store because there are taller buildings in front of it. But it's there." She pointed again. "And over here? That's where your studio is located. I can't see it clearly because there are too many houses in the way. But I've imagined you working late at night, listening to music and painting. Sleeping."

"You don't have to imagine anymore. I'm here, Kathleen. With you."

She reached up and unbuttoned his shirt. Excitement made her clumsy, and her fingers fumbled in their simple task. But when he tried to help her, she pushed his hand away. Her excitement grew with every inch of his flesh that she revealed. Finally, she peeled back the cotton material and beheld his strong, masculine chest. Greedily, she stroked the pattern of chest hair. With light strokes, she teased his flat nipples. He shivered beneath her touch, and she delighted in her power to arouse him.

From somewhere far below them, an ambulance wailed. Life had not ceased. Other people still lived and died and dreamed. But here, on the balcony, time stood still. This was her day, her moment, and she meant to take full advantage of it.

She yanked off his shirt and tossed it inside. She reached for the top button on his Levi's.

"Wait." He caught both her hands in his own. "Turn around."

She faced away from him, her hands braced on the balcony's railing. His light touch caressed her bare shoulders. His lips nuzzled at the nape of her neck, sending shivers up and down her spine. In one swift move, he unzipped her dress. Before Kathleen could catch hold of the bodice, the batik silk had fallen to her waist.

He pressed against her back. His arms encircled her. When he fondled her breasts, she gasped with sheer pleasure. Intense arousal set her senses churning. A delicious aching spread across her skin and sank deep within, permeating her flesh. Her heart thumped hard and fast.

He turned her to face him, but he did not kiss her right away. Instead, he gazed at her. At her eyes, her lips, her naked breasts. Her dress had fallen below her waist and caught on the swell of her hips.

She moistened her lips, forced herself to speak. "You've seen me naked before."

"Not like this."

"I haven't changed shape.

"Before you were a subject." His voice was husky. "A model."

"And now?"

"Now I want to make you mine."

He kissed her breasts, suckled at the taut nipples until she was whimpering with the need for him. He eased her dress off. The blue-and-green material puddled at her feet.

He clasped her tightly against him, and the meeting of their flesh was a grand fulfillment. For a year, she had waited. For a year, she had endured his enmity. For a long, empty year, she had known this was how love must be.

He lifted her in his strong arms and carried her inside. He lowered her to the sheets. His mouth claimed hers.

He stood, tore away his Levi's and came toward her.

"Wait," she said. She'd imagined this moment so many times. "Let me look at you."

She propped herself up for a better view. He was magnificently aroused. So strong. So masculine. She savored the moment. The fascination. Everything about him excited her. His firm torso and flat belly. The pattern of hair on his chest.

"Satisfied?" he asked.

"Not nearly." She stretched out luxuriously on her satin blue sheets. "Make love to me, Foster."

He didn't need a second invitation. He lay beside her, caressed her breasts, her torso, the soft flesh above her knees. And when he touched the moist, intimate folds between her legs, she thought she would faint from pleasure.

He parted her thighs wide, then wider. His first thrust inside her was fierce and strong. And she gasped with animal delight. More, she wanted more.

He plunged again. And again. Driving her higher and higher. She writhed beneath him, clinging to every sensation, imprinting it upon her memory, afraid that this might never happen again. The poignancy of loss intensified her pleasure. When finally he found a hard, fast rhythm, passion consumed her entirely. Sensation exploded behind her eyes. Her body blossomed with fulfillment.

And she was at peace.

They stretched out beside each other, waiting for their breathing to return to normal, waiting for the hammering of their hearts to ease.

The clock beside her bed showed the time to be nearly eleven. Only an hour left in this precious day.

There were a million things she needed to say to him. They needed to discuss the art show and the paintings of her. She needed to tell him about the time merchant and the day she'd bought. But Kathleen was speechless.

Chapter Thirteen

"I want to know," Zach said softly. "Kathleen, I want to know your secret. You promised to tell me before midnight."

She rolled to her stomach, propped her head on the pillow and stared at her oak headboard. The wood was as hard as the reality that blocked her dreams. There was so much to say... and so little time.

If she avoided explanations—which was a very tempting proposition—Kathleen would have no control over the way he learned about her trip through time or her reasons for buying these precious hours. She wouldn't be able to explain because she wouldn't be here. In less than an hour, she would be swept forward one year.

She made her decision. "I want to tell you. Foster, you were right when you said there shouldn't be anything standing between us. This is the truth. The whole truth. But I warn you, it's going to sound a little strange."

A little strange? she mused. That was like saying van Gogh was a little odd. Like calling a tornado a little wind. Like claiming their lovemaking was a little fulfilling. How could he possibly understand?

"I'm waiting," he said.

Second thoughts raced through her. She stretched out full-length, miming the languid relaxation that came with complete satisfaction. "But I feel so lazy."

Maybe he would never need to know about the magic. She had bought only one day, from midnight to midnight. Tomorrow, she would still be here, physically. Why should he know?

But even though she'd had inklings to the contrary, would she somehow revert to being the old Kathleen? The flighty Kathleen? The spoiled princess who had ruined things in the first place? Would her hair grow back to the length before she had cut it? She almost felt sorry for her old self, waking and finding that her life had been drastically altered. Would she forget? Remember? Would she change immediately?

And when she went forward again, would she remember what had happened? An odd sense of loss crept over her. Why, if she and Foster fell in love now, and she promptly returned to the future, she might lose an entire year of happiness. All the tender moments of discovery. A whole year of making love to him. She was almost jealous of her other self, the one who would experience the events that took place between June twenty-first and June twenty-first.

If time turned out well, she reminded herself. There were still no guarantees. He still had not declared his love.

"I don't understand it myself," she finally said honestly.

He rested his hand on her back, encouraging her. Very gently, his fingers made swirling, tingling patterns on her skin. He leaned close to her ear. His breath tickled, triggering fresh sensations within her. "Something important happened here. Between us. I want you to level with me. Because this was more than sex. This was..."

His voice trailed off. What was he about to say? That he loved her? Oh, please, it had to be. "This was...what?"

"I feel different about you now than I did before."

"Different in what way?" She had to know. If she was going to be catapulted into an uncertain future, she needed this moment to cherish, to remember for the rest of her life.

"Different," he said. There was a finality in his tone that precluded further discussion. But he wasn't harsh or stern, and his tender stroking of her back continued. "Explain your magic, Kathleen. Be honest. Not mysterious."

"It began with your paintings," she said. "Today was not the first time I saw them."

"That can't be. Today was the day I finished them."

"The first time I saw them, you hadn't made the changes on the small portrait. Today, you added a rouge color beneath my chin." She recalled the small acrylic modifications. "A dab of white in my eyes. A darker line to my lashes."

"How did you know that?"

"I lived this day before," she said. "The last time I lived June twenty-first, it was the worst day of my life. My mother had a stroke. And I destroyed any sort of relationship that you and I might have shared."

His hand on her back stilled. "And how did you get this second chance?"

"I bought a day. From a woman named Diana Marie Casey."

So far, so good. He wasn't laughing at her or suggesting she seek immediate psychiatric help.

"Assuming this is possible," he said, "why?"

She couldn't tell him that she'd purchased twenty-four hours in order to seduce him into forgiving her, into loving her. Could she? She hedged, "I didn't like the way it turned out the first time."

"How did it turn out?"

He had hated her, despised her. And she had spent a year in misery. But should she mention that?

"Oh, damn." How could he truly love her if she was not completely honest?

Avoiding his gaze, she said, "I was different a year ago than I am right now. More impulsive. Less controlled. You noticed the change right away."

"Yes, I did."

Zachary tried to take these weird revelations seriously. When she'd shown up on his doorstep with her

new haircut and kissed him, he'd felt he was seeing a
new side to Kathleen Welles. But not a new Kathleen!
Not a woman who had lived a year in the future.

Somehow, this story worried him, didn't feel right.
Throughout the day, he'd seen her in action, rearranging other people's lives. Was he simply her latest
project? "When you saw the paintings for the first
time, what happened?"

"I knew they were brilliant."

"Right," he said. "But what happened?"

"I forbade you to show them."

"Not unlike this time," he reminded her. "Al-
though *forbade* is too strong a word. This time you
suggested. And what happened the last time?"

"You wouldn't listen to me."

He studied the curve of her shoulders in the moonlight. The velvet texture of her skin beckoned to him.
And yet, he held back. There was more to her story,
and her reluctance convinced him that there would not
be a happy ending.

"We fought," she said.

"Argued?"

"No, we physically fought. I'm not proud of this,
Foster. I went kind of crazy. I had an X-Acto blade in
my hand. You restrained me." She buried her face in
the pillow, then looked up again. "I think I cracked
one of your ribs."

He knew she had not yet finished her story. "Does
this get worse?"

"I slashed your paintings to ribbons, destroyed them."

His heart thumped in his chest. Her story was fantastic, unbelievable. And yet, he knew she was telling the truth. Somewhere in his mind, he had a memory that hadn't happened. And he felt a dark pain, a wound that had not healed.

"You could never forgive me," she said.

"That would be true," he said. There was a cold, hard knot in the pit of his stomach. "I couldn't forgive such desecration."

"But you know how I feel about the paintings," she said. "I know they're as wonderful as the masterpieces that surrounded us tonight. But if they're displayed here in Denver, I'll feel humiliated. People will gossip behind my back. And I need to maintain their respect for me as a businesswoman."

She shuddered. "To be naked before my whole world seems unbearable."

"I can't understand this, Kathleen. We're not talking about a sleazy porno magazine. These are works of art. People who snicker at art are childish jerks. The kind of people who giggle at bare breasts in *National Geographic*. Why the hell would you care what they think?"

"I don't know, Foster. But I can't ignore my position. I'm going to be acting president at Welles. I can't start this new job with a scandal."

He withdrew his hand from her back, and she was painfully torn. She wanted to be with him, to please him, to love him. And yet, those paintings might destroy her.

Slowly, he said, "So you came back in time, you went through this whole complicated scheme, you got me into bed. And the whole purpose was so you wouldn't be embarrassed."

"No," she protested. "That's not it at all."

The whole purpose, the whole reason for being here, was to save her mother and to give herself and Zachary Foster a chance at lasting love. She turned on her side, tried to look into his eyes. But he was staring straight ahead. She could feel herself losing him.

Desperately, she recounted, "When we were in the museum, I had a vision. It was just a glimpse. But so vivid that I recall every detail."

"You had one, too?"

She sat up, pulled the sheets up to cover her breasts and stared at him. "Have you had these visions?"

"Twice today. I told you about the first one, when I saw the woman you call Diana Marie."

"I don't know what it means." Helplessly, she gestured. Her decision to relive this day must have thrown time off-kilter, releasing dozens of time bubbles. Past. Present. Future. Glimpses into what would be. Or what might be. "Unless it's like a flashback that hasn't yet happened."

"A flash-forward," he said. "What did you see?"

"Myself. I was very old. My face was lined with wrinkles. I had a long white braid hanging down my back. And I stood in a museum of some sort. I saw a long hallway with a row of paintings displayed. I'm sure I've never been to this place before." She realized that he was staring at her. "Do you think I'm crazy?"

"I was imagining what you'd look like as an old woman. Dignified and beautiful." He fought the icy anger that had started in his belly. He didn't want to hate her. He was very close to the opposite. "I don't want to lose you, Kathleen."

Suppressed emotion caught at her throat, choking her. She didn't want to lose him, either. Why would he think such a thing? She would never leave him. As long as he wanted her, she would be with him.

"What else did you see in your vision?"

"I was alone." She forced herself to speak. Her words seemed heavy with portent, as if she were condemning herself to a future without him. "You weren't with me, Foster, and I felt so lonesome, so bereft."

"What else?" he asked.

"I stood before your large painting of me. It was displayed prominently, lit with spotlights. Treasured."

"I'll be damned." That future was something he had hoped for but never expected. He wanted recognition and respect, but he knew better than to plan for it. "I might like this magic of yours. At least, some of it. I don't suppose your vision predicted whether I would display the paintings of you at the gallery opening tomorrow, did it?"

"I can't make that decision, Foster."

"I know."

He'd be a royal bastard to show the studies, knowing how she felt. When he had stood in front of them in his studio, knife poised to slash the canvases, he knew that was the only way. He had to destroy them. Otherwise, he wasn't sure he could prevent himself from showing his best work.

He had raised the knife. Actually touched the razor-sharp edge to canvas.

But he couldn't bring himself to do it.

Slashing the paintings would have been like destroying a piece of himself. And of Kathleen. He couldn't do it. But to keep them and not show them? Such a plan required superhuman self-control. But he had to. Had to hold himself back. He couldn't betray her.

She trusted him. Lying there, so beautiful and sweet, she had placed her future in his hands. As he looked at her, the coldness left him. Though she said he had hated her, he could not allow that feeling to take root and grow. He couldn't hurt her. It would be better to take a blade and chop off his own right hand than to cause her a moment's pain or regret. "You said we fought," he said, "the last time you lived this day. Is that right?"

"Yes."

"And you cracked one of my ribs?"

"I'm sorry, Foster."

"Let's have that be the last time we hurt each other, okay?"

"I'd like that. I'll never hurt you again."

He didn't bother pointing out that she hadn't done it the first time. Whatever had happened before had changed.

"I had a second vision," he said. "It was when we were looking for Chad and Angela in the church. Out of the corner of my eye, I saw you." He cleared his throat. "You were dressed like a bride."

That was a future he hadn't contemplated. Marriage hadn't been on his agenda, hadn't been one of his plans.

Not that he wasn't fascinated by Kathleen. Not that their lovemaking hadn't been the most fantastic sensual experience of his life. But marriage?

"A bride," she murmured with that wistful longing women sometimes got. "Was I beautiful?"

He remembered her face through the veil. Vivacious. Excited. Her lips poised on the brink of laughter. "Very."

"Tell me this, Foster. Hypothetically, if I were your bride would you still want to display those paintings?"

"Married or not, it wouldn't make a difference to me. It's the best work I've ever done, Kathleen. It kills me not to show it to the world. But I won't display them because I don't want to hurt you."

He collapsed back on the pillows. The temptation to bring those paintings to the gallery was enormous. And even if he managed to get past this particular showing without displaying them, he would still want to share them with his fellow artists and art lovers. He couldn't trust himself to keep them a secret forever. He would have to destroy them.

But he couldn't do that, either.

"I have an idea, Kathleen. *You* take the portraits."

"What?"

"One of them is rightfully yours, anyway. This whole thing started because you commissioned me to do a portrait."

"But I haven't paid you."

"Now you can." He climbed from the bed and pulled on his Levi's. "For the magnificent sum of one dollar, all three paintings are yours to do with as you wish. Chop them up in to little pieces. Hide them in the back of your closet. I don't care. I'm going to entrust them to you."

"Right now?"

"We'd better do it now before I come to my senses." He stuck his arms into his sleeves. "Come on, Kathleen."

She stared at her digital clock until the numbers burned into her eyes. Eleven-fourteen. Only forty-six minutes left in her day. She wanted to make love again. She wanted to hold him, to pull him through time with her.

He stood over her, leaned down and kissed her once on the mouth. His tongue teased but did not penetrate. "Let's go, princess. I made you an offer you can't refuse."

"I want to stay here with you. I want to make love to you again before the day is over." She caught hold of his arm and pulled him down on the bed beside her. "Foster, I don't know what's going to happen at midnight. But that's the end of the day I bought. I'm going to go forward in time again."

He gently pushed the hair off her forehead. "At the magical hour of midnight? The witching hour?"

"You don't take this seriously," she accused.

"I take you very seriously. What you believe is important to me."

"But you don't believe there was a time merchant."

"Oh, yeah, there was. I saw her in one of those weird flashes of vision. But I don't believe you're going to vanish in a puff of smoke. You're real, Kathleen." He held her hand to his mouth and nipped.

"Ouch!"

"See? You have real sensations. Your body isn't a dream or a vision. You're here. And you'll stay here. With me."

"Kiss me, Foster." He didn't understand. The minutes were vanishing. And she would be gone. Near desperation, she pleaded, "Make love to me again."

"I will." He pulled away from her. "But not right now. My darling princess, you're not going anywhere. I won't let you. I'll hold you so nothing can take you away from me."

She wanted to believe he was stronger than magic, that his strength could hold back time. But she feared it was not so.

"I'll make love to you," he promised. "At one minute after midnight."

But she would not be here! A sense of regret and loss, deeper than anything she'd felt before, overwhelmed her. Before she had bought these hours and experienced the lovemaking she'd dreamed about for so many lonely nights, she had not known what she was missing. But now? She couldn't imagine living without him.

She fought back her tears. No, she wouldn't waste these precious moments crying.

"Come on," he urged. "You came back in time to take care of those paintings. Let's do it."

She threw on a pair of shorts and a T-shirt. The minutes were ticking away. When they went to the parking lot below the building, the clock in her car showed only twenty-eight minutes left.

Ten minutes to his studio. Another four to get out of the car and inside his carriage house. Fourteen minutes left.

Foster wrapped the paintings. Two minutes for each.

At exactly eight minutes until midnight, he placed them in the back of her car and slammed the door. "They're yours."

Kathleen should have felt pleased. She'd achieved her many goals for this day. Her mother was saved from the agony of a stroke. The paintings were intact but not going into the showing. She'd seduced Foster, had experienced the exquisite pleasure of his most intimate touch.

It was only now that she realized she still hadn't accomplished the most important task for the day.

He had not stated his love for her. He had not said the words that would bind him to her for all eternity. And she had only seven minutes left to convince him.

"The reason I came back and relived this day was you." Urgency made her tense, but she had not one second to spare. She needed to be clear, needed to be certain. In the moonlight outside his studio, she took his hands. She gazed up at him, memorizing his features. She might never see him this way again. In the interval of a year, so much could happen.

She caressed his cheek, roughened by twenty-four hours' worth of beard. And she melted into his arms. Her lips joined with his for one last tender, poignant kiss.

Was this goodbye forever? Her pulse raced. Her body trembled with remembered sensations from their lovemaking. She looked up into his eyes.

"I love you." More loudly, she repeated, "I love you, Zachary Foster. And I always will. Throughout time. No matter what else happens, I love you."

"My beautiful Kathleen."

He smiled, and the light from his blue eyes shone into her open, vulnerable heart. "Say it," she demanded. "Please, Foster. The time is almost gone. Please, say it."

"My beautiful, crazy Kathleen. My darling, I—"

It was midnight.

Though she clung to him, she was no longer in his arms. The mists came over her like a sudden shroud, veiling her, obscuring her vision. "No!" she screamed. "Not yet. No!"

But the magic was upon her. Though she could not feel her arms or legs, she was fighting furiously. Like being caught in a nightmare and struggling to awaken, pulling aside layers of darkness, one after another. Always finding one more layer.

The web of time tangled around her. She heard the high winds, felt the lash of rains and the heat of sun. Crazily, the world revolved kaleidoscopically. Shards of vision flashed before her like those in a broken mirror. She saw Diana Marie as Mrs. van Winkle, as the chauffeur, as herself. She heard her mother's voice, telling her that everything would be all right. Father Blaize beckoned to her. Dr. Mathers swung his golf club.

Then all the pieces settled. She felt pavement beneath her feet. She felt the summer sun beating down on her shoulders. It was midday. June twenty-first. Kathleen wore the black jersey dress. She stood outside the building where she'd first encountered the time merchant. Above her, the stone gargoyles smirked in grotesque amusement.

She was back!

Chapter Fourteen

Kathleen glanced at her wristwatch. It was one-thirty in the afternoon, only a few moments after she'd first met Diana Marie. Automatically, Kathleen tensed, thinking of all that must be done. Then she relaxed, remembering that there was no longer a need to rush frantically. The hours stretched endlessly before her. There would be a tomorrow. And a day after that. Never before had time seemed like such a luxury.

Unfortunately, now that she had all the time in the world, she had no memory. How had this past year turned out? What had happened? Though she vividly remembered the June twenty-first she had just lived, she had no recollection of a changed year. All she could recall was the agonizing year she'd already lived. Foster's hatred. Her mother's struggle.

Life was different now, she thought. Or was it? Had she fantasized the whole thing?

Hoping to find an explanation, she turned toward the building where Diana Marie had first made her magic and where she had later appeared as Mrs. van

Winkle. The door was boarded shut. The upstairs windows were filthy and dark. No one home, Kathleen thought. The time merchant had moved on.

The clock sign Foster had designed was nowhere in evidence. This address was nothing more than a decrepit warehouse in downtown Denver, probably soon destined to become a parking lot for the new baseball stadium.

Slowly, she walked along the street, searching for a clue that the world was different now. Her path led to Kendall Gallery.

When she entered, a tall, bearded man, the owner, swooped down upon her. "Kathleen Welles!" he enthused. "Good to see you."

"And you, too." She had no idea what his name was.

"So are you coming to the showing this weekend?"

"Wouldn't miss it."

"After last year's success, I decided to make it an annual thing. The spring show for local talent."

A portrait prominently displayed in the front window caught her eye. With the incredible, mesmerizing aura of light and dark across the man's face and shoulders, she didn't need to ask the name of the artist. Zachary Foster had created this piece. The subject was Father Blaize.

"Don't you love that piece?" the gallery owner enthused. He rubbed his hands together, mantislike. "It's already sold, but I wanted to show it."

"Who bought it?" she asked.

"It was a doctor. Mathers is his name. Greg Mathers. A nice guy. Hell of a golfer."

Kathleen eased toward the exit. "Well, I guess I'll see you on the weekend."

"Sure. Drop by anytime. Bring your friends."

My rich friends, she thought as she returned to the street. From the little she knew about the gallery owner, he was still the same. A good, acquisitive salesman.

She rode the shuttle bus down the Sixteenth Street Mall to Welles. And the sameness of the building comforted her. Apparently, nothing ghastly, such as a buyout or a bankruptcy, had occurred during her missing year. As she meandered through the displays on her way to the elevators, she couldn't see any difference. Until she reached the shoe department.

"Mother?"

Hannah stood by a display, holding a red shoe in one hand and a black one in the other. "Kathleen, darling. I'm so glad you're here."

Not as glad as Kathleen. Her mother was vibrant with health. Her cheeks were tanned. Her posture erect. And her hair was newly styled in a casual, no-care sweep. Her eyes sparkled with an enthusiasm Kathleen had not seen for many years.

"Which one?" Hannah held out the shoes. "I need something for that red-and-black sundress I bought for my vacation in Rio. Now this shade of red is perfect. But the style of the black is more casual."

"Get both," Kathleen said. She wanted to gather her mother in her arms and hug her. "Either way, you'll be gorgeous."

"Not too gorgeous, I hope," her shopping companion said. "When she came with us on the Alaska cruise, Greg and I had to beat the men away from her with a stick."

Kathleen recognized Gregory Mathers's wife. "How are you, Clarice?"

"Never better. I love shopping with your mother. She has such wonderful taste."

Remembering her stop at the gallery, Kathleen said, "Tell me about the portrait your husband bought. The one by Zachary Foster."

"The priest," Clarice said. She glanced over Kathleen's shoulder and beamed. "Greg's here. Ask him yourself."

Kathleen turned and looked up into the doctor's smiling face. Though he had not significantly changed in a physical sense, there was a difference in Dr. Mathers. She saw a gentleness, a thoughtfulness, that had not been there before.

"Hi, Kathleen. You saw the painting of Father Blaize?"

She nodded.

While her mother and Clarice delved more deeply into the mysteries of shoes, he spoke to her in a firm, level voice that automatically inspired great confidence.

"After that day..." he said. "It was exactly a year ago, wasn't it?"

"Yes, it was." She waited on the brink of anticipation, certain Dr. Mathers was going to tell her about that day, going to offer proof that she had relived the twenty-first of June.

"Anyway, after you and Zachary Foster taught me my job by dragging me off a golf course at gunpoint—well, I guess I should say at fake gunpoint—" He stopped, studying her. "You don't look well, Kathleen."

"I don't?" She had clutched the edge of a shoe display to keep her knees from buckling. Her day *had* occurred. She hadn't dreamed it or fantasized it.

"When was the last time you were in for a checkup?"

"I don't recall," she said, quite honestly. "It could have been anytime in the past year." She straightened. "Please go on."

"Well, I had a lot of questions about myself. My ethics. The reasons I went into medicine in the first place. Because you knew so firmly that your mother would be stricken, and there was no scientific explanation, I remembered something very important. Human beings are more than pieces and parts put together like clockworks."

She liked this man a lot better than the golf-playing doctor she'd met a year ago.

He continued. "Given two patients with almost identical symptoms, one might survive while the other dies. Why? Why can't physicians patch and suture and expect identical results?" He frowned. "I went looking for answers, and I met Father Blaize at a fundraising banquet for Mercy Hospital. You were there."

"I remember," Kathleen said.

"A wise, compassionate man. But practical, too. I wanted that portrait as a reminder that there's more to medicine than mechanics. I've worked with the human heart, but it's only in the past year that I've learned the heart is more than a muscle."

Thus far, Kathleen was well pleased with the results of her changed day. She went upstairs to the office of the acting president. Herself. In the outer area, she stopped at Helen's desk. "What's on my schedule for the afternoon?"

"Meetings at three, three-thirty and four. Did you take care of that problem with the window dressers?"

A chill went through her. This particular scenario was much too similar to the way it had been the last time she'd lived this day. "A problem with the window dressers? With Zachary Foster?"

"Foster and his gang of thugs," Helen said. "You mustn't forget to discuss their grooming."

Kathleen went into her office, closed the door and leaned against it. If Foster hated her, if she had not managed to strike a spark of love in the muscle of his heart, she didn't know how she could stand it.

A dark cloud of failure fogged her mind as she thought beyond the past twenty-four hours to the year when he'd despised her. Had she done something foolish to earn his hatred? Perhaps it was fated. Perhaps their love was not to be.

A silent cry caught in her throat, pierced her soul. Now, she loved him more deeply than ever. Though they'd made love a year ago in actual time, that passion was only a few moments old in her memory. She needed his touch. She could not live without his love.

She remembered the last time Helen had advised her there was a problem with the window designers. Kathleen had confronted Foster, who'd coldly demanded real diamonds instead of costume jewelry. And she had promised to meet with him at two o'clock.

It was two o'clock now. If she went to the large display window in the front of the store, she knew she would find him waiting. But what else could she expect?

Would she see hatred in his eyes? Would she hear the harsh tones of disgust in his baritone voice? Unfortunately, there was only one way to find out. Gathering every shred of courage she possessed, Kathleen flung open her office door.

"Helen, would you please reschedule—"

"Your appointments for the afternoon." The secretary cocked her head. "Are you all right?"

"I'll let you know later. Right now, I'll be ..."

She waited for Helen to complete the sentence, but her secretary said nothing. Kathleen continued. "I'll be in the front display, talking with Foster."

"Very well, dear. Good luck."

It was fear and not courage that quickened her steps through the store. In the narrow corridor behind the front window, she met Donny. "Whoa, Kathleen," he said. "Somebody chasing you?"

The past, she thought. She was being pursued by demons she couldn't recognize but knew well enough to fear. "How are you, Donny?"

"Cool." He bobbed his head. "Way cool."

She tried to achieve a similar coolness as she asked, "And your brother, Chad? And Angela? How are they doing?"

His look was puzzled. "You saw them two days ago."

"Of course." She snapped her fingers as if recalling a memory that had slipped her mind. "Silly me. They're doing fine since Angela doesn't have to live with that monster, Royce."

"You got that right," he said. He slipped past her. "Hey, Foster's waiting out there in the window."

"Is he?" Her nerves drew taut.

"Bye," Donny said. "Stay cool."

Great advice. If only she could follow it.

Kathleen eased around the edge of the display. She had never in her life been so utterly terrified. Her knees were shaking. She felt dizzy.

He had his back to her. In his sleeveless T-shirt, his bare shoulders glistened. He sensed her presence. "Kathleen? About those diamonds..."

Oh, no. Nothing had changed. Somehow, during the year she could not remember, she had destroyed their relationship. Despite all her efforts, despite their lovemaking, he had come to despise her.

He continued. "Too many diamonds in this display would be tacky. I only need one perfect stone."

Her head drooped. Her eyes downcast, she couldn't bear to look at him, to see the hatred in his expression. Her hands fell lifeless to her sides. It was over. She'd had a second chance and had failed. In a dull, exhausted voice, she said, "I'll arrange for it."

"I've already taken care of it."

By the sound of his voice, she could tell that he'd come closer. His hands clasped her shoulders, and she felt his warmth, his tenderness. His love? Her eyelids snapped open. She stared into his face. His eyes were beacons, glowing with sensitive concern.

"Foster, do you..."

"I love you, princess. With all my heart."

The words clanged, loud as a carillon. He loved her! "Do you? Tell me again."

A quirky smile turned up one corner of his mouth. "I've been telling you that every single day. For exactly one year. When are you going to believe me?"

She didn't know whether to cry from relief or to laugh with pleasure. She eased against him, settling into his embrace. "I've missed so much," she said. "An entire year with you."

"Sure, princess." He stroked her hair. "Whatever you say."

"Are you patronizing me?"

"I'm indulging you. It's a skill, and I'm getting pretty proficient at it."

There was so much to catch up on. A year's worth of conversations she had not heard. All those hours of making love. The sweet experiences of a first year in love. She would miss that time. But the result was well worth the loss. "Love eternal," she said.

"About these diamonds," he said. "I came up with something different."

With his arm around her waist, he guided her to the front window so she could observe the full effect of the display.

An amazed laugh bubbled up inside her, effervescent as champagne. "It's Diana Marie."

The mannequin wore a wig of long, wild hair. And scarves, dozens of scarves. A gauzy skirt. A ton of costume jewelry. Behind her was an hourglass. As Kathleen watched, the hourglass swung in a circle, and the glistening sands again filtered through.

"Mechanized," Foster said. "Pretty nifty, huh?"

"I love it," she said. "But I don't see any diamonds."

"Sit right here."

He gestured to a low velvet bench and waited until she had settled herself. Then he went down on one knee before her. In his hand, he held a small velvet box. He flipped open the lid and revealed a perfect diamond ring.

"Kathleen, will you marry me?"

In the periphery of her gaze, she saw the mannequin, whose resemblance to Diana Marie was un-
canny. And she saw something more.

Nighttime in a park. She and Foster walked beside
a lake. The moonlight made brilliant reflections across
its dark surface more wonderful than a Monet painting.

In her mind, she heard his voice, echoing as if from
afar, whispering, "I love you. My princess, I love
you."

Then they were in sunlight, surrounded with flowers, exotically scented blooms, selecting a bouquet.

Time bubbles, Kathleen thought. Popping through
her mind.

She saw herself and Foster in the bedroom of her
condominium, quietly holding hands after making
love. The decor was different. Simpler, more mod-
ern. On the wall above her bed hung the three nude
paintings. The paintings! They were there, hers, un-
displayed until she chose the right moment.

And Foster spoke to her of inspiration, of how the
existence of his masterpieces inspired him to create
more fluidly and brilliantly than ever before.

In the blink of an eye, the sounds and the visions
faded. But Kathleen knew they were not gone forever. She would experience her memories of times she
did not know. She had not lost a minute...she'd only
misplaced them.

Her mind returned to the present, to this special
moment. She looked down at Foster, the most hand-

some, talented, sensitive, strong, brave man she'd ever known. Her lover.

Her husband?

She sighed. Life was good.

"Kathleen," he said, "we're drawing a crowd."

Outside, several pedestrians had stopped to stare at the tableau in the front window of Welles. When she looked out, Kathleen saw her mother smiling and nodding approval. Dr. Gregory Mathers and his wife also observed. And Donny, grinning so wide she thought his face would split.

At the edge of the crowd, Kathleen caught a glimpse of a woman with dark, intelligent eyes. Then she was gone.

"Kathleen," Foster repeated, "will you marry me?"

"I love you, Zachary Foster. Yes, I will marry you."

He slipped the engagement ring onto her finger.

Through the window, she saw people applauding. She rose to her feet, facing him. He stood.

And their lips joined in a kiss, sealing their vow of eternal love.

HARLEQUIN®

A M E R I C A N ◆ R O M A N C E®

Once in a while, there's a story so special, a story so unusual,
that your pulse races, your blood rushes. We call this

TO HEAVEN AND BACK is one such book.

Danny Johnson doesn't know a good thing when he sees it.
Callie Moran is the perfect woman for him, but after losing his
fiancée a year ago, he can't look another beautiful woman in
the eye. Some celestial intervention is called for, and Jason and
Sabrina are just the pair to do it. Don't miss this companion to
HEAVEN KNOWS.

TO HEAVEN AND BACK
by
Tracy Hughes

Available in April, wherever Harlequin books are sold.
Watch for more Heartbeat stories, coming your way soon!

Fifty red-blooded, white-hot, true-blue hunks
from every State in the Union!

Look for MEN MADE IN AMERICA! Written by some
of our most popular authors, these stories feature some
of the strongest, sexiest men, each from a different state
in the union!

Two titles available every month at your favorite
retail outlet.

In March, look for:

UNEASY ALLIANCE by Jayne Ann Krentz (Oregon)
TOO NEAR THE FIRE by Lindsay McKenna (Ohio)

In April, look for:

FOR THE LOVE OF MIKE by Candace Schuler (Texas)
THE DEVLIN DARE by Cathy Thacker (Virginia)

You won't be able to resist MEN MADE IN AMERICA!

HARLEQUIN®

AMERICAN ROMANCE®

In Name Only

With the advent of spring, American Romance is pleased to be presenting three exciting couples, each with their own unique reasons for needing a new beginning...for needing to enter into a marriage of convenience.

Meet the reluctant newlyweds in:

#580 MARRIAGE, INCORPORATED
Debbie Rawlins
April 1995

#583 THE RUNAWAY BRIDE
Jacqueline Diamond
May 1995

#587 A SHOTGUN WEDDING
Cathy Gillen Thacker
June 1995

Find out why some couples marry first...and learn to love later. Watch for the upcoming In Name Only promotion.

INO-1

IS BRINGING
YOU A BABY BOOM!

NEW ARRIVALS

We're expecting! Over this spring, from March through May, three very special Harlequin American Romance authors invite you to read about three equally special heroines—all of whom are on a nine-month adventure! We expect each soon-to-be mom will find the man of her dreams—and a daddy in the bargain!

So don't miss the next title:

> #579 WHO'S THE DADDY?
> by Judy Christenberry
> April 1995

Look for the New Arrivals logo—and please help us welcome our new arrivals!

NA-1R

Harlequin invites you to the most
romantic wedding of the season.

Rope the cowboy of your dreams in
Marry Me, Cowboy!

A collection of 4 brand-new stories,
celebrating weddings, written by:

New York Times bestselling author

JANET DAILEY

and favorite authors

Margaret Way
Anne McAllister
Susan Fox

Be sure not to miss Marry Me, Cowboy!
coming this April

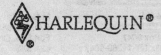HARLEQUIN®

MMC